Welcome HOME

Rita Rumgay

Jan-Carol
Publishing, Inc

"every story needs a book"

Welcome Home
Rita Rumgay
Published March 2023
Little Creek Books
Imprint of Jan-Carol Publishing, Inc
All rights reserved
Copyright © 2023 by Rita Rumgay

ISBN: 978-1-954978-84-3
Library of Congress Control Number: 2023934420

You may contact the publisher:
Jan-Carol Publishing, Inc
PO Box 701
Johnson City, TN 37605
publisher@jancarolpublishing.com
www.jancarolpublishing.com

To those that know the struggles of life.

I see you.

Author's Note

Dear Reader,

As you read *Welcome Home*, I hope you can relate to some of the characters. Maybe you will recognize yourself or someone you know. Mostly, my wish is for you to laugh more than you cry. Enjoy the ride and happy reading.

Your friend,
Rita Rumgay

Chapter 1

While washing the supper dishes, I think, *Didn't I just do this?* Jake and the children had long left the table, cell phones in hand. As I move the suds in a circular motion over our chipped plates, my mind drifts back to when these dishes were new and we were just starting our family. Our suppers with little Brian and Cindy were so animated. They were excited to share their day. Jake and I would laugh with them, enjoying every word and expression on the cherub faces.

Now the evening meal is just a feeding station that interrupts the things they would rather be doing. If I try to engage anyone into conversation, it's an unwanted distraction.

I tried the "no electronic devices" rule; it lasted maybe two meals. They were so bored and angry, eating quickly as possible in fear of missing one text or tweet. I don't know who these people are any more. They have evolved into strangers.

Both of my children have adopted a new name, a new identity. Cindy, at birth, was named Cynthia; isn't that a pretty name? She is now called "Cin" of all things. Brian now goes by "B-man" to his friends. Upon asking the progressive teenagers why the name change and how that came to be, I get a shoulder shrug or a grunt. In other words, *Butt out, Mom.* When trying to discuss these new identities of our children with my husband, he is irritated at being taken away from his laptop, his work. He then barks that I'm overreacting, again.

When I was a teenager, I remember entertaining the idea of a different name. A name that sounded exotic or classy appealed to me. But here I am, just plain old Ann, not even as interesting as Anne with an E. I do have a middle name, Lynn, but no one ever uses it. When I asked my parents—very religious people, they are—why the plain names, they responded with an explanation of wanting me to maintain humility in my character. So, not to disappoint, I am resigned to a simple, humble name.

My coworkers aren't terribly interested in anything to do with my family. They are all from another generation. With the exception of birthing my children, I have been employed by the same law firm since my twenties. Back then, I was fresh out of community college. A paralegal, beginning my career. After meeting my husband, Jake Cantrell, who needed legal advice for his contracting business, I knew my life was all laid out for me.

The plan was simple: marry Jake, buy a home, go to law school, establish myself in the firm, and then have beautiful babies. All of that would naturally come with the enormous house, built by Jake's company, of course. We would have a pool and a nanny for the children. Jake and I would be the cliché power couple.

Great plan, huh? I guess God was laughing out loud. Apparently, that's what He does when we are making plans.

The dream became a harsh reality. First came the unexpected Cynthia, then a hurried wedding at the courthouse, then a rental home, and then Brian. I barely finished college, never made it to law school. It was daycare for the kids while I worked to help Jake build his business. We have a home in the suburbs that we have re-mortgaged to keep said business afloat. So much for the big plan. We were never wealthy, but we didn't do without food, shelter, or electricity.

As for my job, the firm is now in the hands of the son. His father passed away with a heart attack several years back. I think the son is keeping me on because of a promise to his dad. My days at the firm are surely numbered.

I don't get this generation. There is no urgency, no digging deep, putting in long hours to put the case together and make a solid argument for the client. No one goes out to lunch together. They are all on the latest diet craze and exercise regimen. They run 10Ks, for crying out loud. The last thing I ran was speed shopping at the grocery store to avoid being late for one of the children's events at school.

So, I am now a fact finder. Mostly, I do background checks and data entry. It's all very dry, dull stuff.

I remember a saying: the best things in life are free, or something like that. I think it refers to love, laughter, maybe air and sunshine. Where did my joy go? I used to laugh so hard my face would hurt. I can't remember the last time that happened.

Sure, there are things a person could do, like maybe a change of scenery, a new hairdo, some new clothes, lose weight, read a good book, make a new friend, blah, blah, blah. I have rearranged furniture, scrubbed my house to sparkle and shine, revamped my closet, gotten a makeover, all the above. There's still something missing . . . an emptiness.

My husband's response to the new me is, "Oh, you look nice." Then back to his computer.

I wonder if he would have even noticed if I hadn't asked the question, "Do you see anything different about me?"

Maybe I should have been more patient, but three days had gone by, and I couldn't hold it in another minute.

The response from the dear offspring of my loins was, "Eh," and a shoulder shrug from the boy and, "Whoa, Mom, you should dress your age" from the girl's judgmental face. Yep, not much to laugh about around here.

Have you ever wanted a do-over, a second chance at restarting your life? Do you ask yourself, how did I end up here? Just like frustrated teenagers, sometimes a mom wants to run away from home. What would happen if the expectant husband and ungrateful kids had to do all the laundry, wash the dishes, cook all the meals, and find their own constantly lost things? This mom is ready to bust out of here, leave that dead-end job, and escape the chaotic and frustrating home to find laughter, excitement, peace, and maybe myself, whoever that is now.

The last time I remember complete happiness was the summer vacations with my cousins at my Aunt Millie's. We worked and played hard all summer. I miss the wide-open space and freedom of the long, hot days. After chores, we headed to the lake, splashing and laughing so hard our sides hurt. Then we would sun ourselves on a rock like lazy reptiles.

I feel like a car with a dead battery, desperately in need of a jump start. It's time to push the reset button on my life! All I need is a plan.

Things I need to do, a.k.a., The Plan:
- Start turning household items (junk in the garage and attic) back into money
- Put every extra dime into my (secret) savings account
- Go through all my personal items (burn some), just keep what I can take with me
- Cancel life insurance (wouldn't want the husband to hunt me down later)

Well, that's a start. I'll add more as I think of what I might need for my getaway.

It may take me a while to make it happen, but I'm feeling better just getting a list made.

Chapter 2

It's a bright Monday morning, and I have a plan. I didn't waste any energy on my family. I was up and out the door before they were out of bed. Let them take care of their own breakfast. Let the husband remind them to turn in homework—yeah, like that's going to happen. Either way, they will need to learn independence very, very soon. Might as well start now.

After arriving at work, I submerged myself in just that—work. I didn't engage anyone, no longer trying to make friends with the millennial people. I know they want me gone, so I'm keeping my head down. I just need a little longer to save up enough starting-over money.

Just as a side bar, I feel like I should explain the secret savings account. My mother, bless her heart, wasn't the lovey-dovey type . . . You know, cuddles and kisses when you get a boo boo, long talks, having a girls day with shopping and lunch. She was rigid and distant; just do as you are told, and there won't be trouble. But she did give me some excellent advice when it came to money—"Start putting back a little at time. No one needs to know about it. A woman needs to have a financial safety net, just in case."

You must imagine this advice with a stern, straight-in-the-eye look from her neatly made-up face and bouffant hairdo.

I heeded her warning and have a tidy sum to my name only. She and I have never spoken of it again and probably never will. We don't share personal information.

At the end of the day, one of the girls (we'll call her Fake Fran—acrylic nails and silicone eyelashes) asked me, "What's the deal with you?" I just smiled my most sarcastic smile, which went right over her head, and replied, "Just dealing with it, baby." She made as much of a frown as her Botox injections would allow. I must really be behaving differently for her to notice. So, I've gone a little crazy. I think I'm due.

After my bumper-to-bumper drive home, I made myself a sandwich while listening to my children slamming doors, having your basic teenage temper tantrum, all because there wasn't a three-course meal served to them. They know where the kitchen is. They have two hands.

I almost caved, had to give myself a talking to in the bathroom mirror. The wet towels on the floor, left since this morning, helped me get past giving in and being Mommy again. Besides, I have work to do. There is an attic and a garage full of assets that awaits claiming.

I started in the garage, making designated piles: leave behind, turn into money, and kick to the curb. In the middle of my finding baby things, the husband arrives home.

"What's for dinner, Hon?"

I reply, "Whatever you want to fix yourself." I turned back to my work. I'm not sure how long he stood there, staring at me.

Busy into my separating, I noticed it started getting dark. So, I switched the light on. A little after that, a pizza delivery man was ringing the bell at the front door. Jake's "What's for dinner?" problem was solved. I thought there would be a barrage of questions. What's going on, why aren't you cooking, have you lost your mind? But, no, maybe I won't even be missed after all.

After my shower, I decided to sleep on the sofa. That would be my new bed until my departure day. It's not like there was anything going on in the bedroom anyway, not for quite some time. I used to think maybe he was having an affair. Now, I don't know that I care. When did he stop kissing me goodbye in the morning, hello in the afternoon, and goodnight at bedtime? Did I stop or was it him? Somewhere in there, we became roommates instead of a couple. It doesn't matter now. I've got a plan. As long as I stick to the plan, I will be happy again. I just know it.

Tomorrow, I'll put in for what is left of my vacation time, and since we haven't taken a vacation in several years, I probably have at least a month's worth saved up. I don't know why I didn't think of that before. That will be plenty of time to get all the things finished up here.

I'm a little excited. A new start. Now, let's see, where would I like to live if I could live anywhere I wanted? Do I want to live in the country, or in the city? I know the suburbs are out, and I know I don't want to live in an apartment building.

Maybe a little cottage on a country lane would be a nice place to live. I can just picture it, ivy growing on the chimney, a babbling brook just a short walk away through the forest. It sounds like something in a Disney movie.

Back to reality, Ann, you need something you can manage. Which means, you will need a job that will support you and your new life, or it's probably going to be a mobile home in a trailer park for you.

No, that's thinking too small, I need to be thinking condo. Yes, that's probably doable.

Add to list: check real-estate listings for future home.

I set the alarm on my phone for 6:00 a.m. to assure that I will be long gone in the morning before the family gets up. Avoiding negativity much? You bet!

Chapter 3

My family thinks I have lost my mind. They tried to stage an intervention. It was so cute the way the children tried to convince me that they were legitimately concerned about my wellbeing. Even Jake almost broke down. Well, his eyes sparkled a little. Might have been a tear. The whole scene lasted no longer than 15 minutes before they gave up trying to understand my about face on motherhood and marital duties. I know how long it took because of the clock on the wall just above their collective heads. Concentrating on its swinging pendulum kept me from raging at them.

After they had given up trying to change me back, I sat on the sofa, realizing no one had offered to clean the house, cook the food, do the laundry, or the hundreds of other menial tasks I once performed. They just wanted to know why I had quit on them. Didn't I know that they had needs? Why didn't I care about them anymore? In other words, it was all about them. I was informed in no uncertain terms that it was my job to take care of them. *Oh, what, oh, what are we to do with MOTHER? She's acting so weird.*

I didn't expect much from Cindy and Brian. But Jake, you would think he would miss me a little. There was a time we couldn't be in the same room without being next to each other, holding hands and talking about anything and everything.

But there he was, shaking his head at me. I was keeping him from somewhere he'd rather be, from something he'd rather be doing.

In a calm, soft voice, I tried to explain that I'm not boycotting them, I just want them to step up, to be more independent. Soon, they would be out in the big bad world and wouldn't even know how to make a grilled cheese sandwich or do a load of laundry. Bottom line—it's time for them to start taking care of themselves.

Anger ensued. They all left the room with the last words being, "Unbelievable, whatever" from Cin, "What a load of crap," from the B man, and, "You must be going through a midlife crisis," from the husband.

I couldn't help thinking, *I thought they'd never leave.* This actually made me laugh, a sound that was so unfamiliar that it didn't sound like me. Oh, well, I've an attic to go through. Onward and upward.

After ascending the fold-down steps, I could tell there wouldn't be much to sell from there. It was mostly Christmas decorations and tax records. There was nothing I wanted to take with me or needed to toss.

The next few days went about like this: Get up, fold sofa-bed covers, do hygiene, dress and feed self, sell items online, search real-estate for new home, avoid family, repeat.

On Sunday, we went to church, just as we always do. Brian and Cynthia went off with the youth to do their worship time. Jake and I sat together, just like always. The only difference being, on the drive home, he asked, "When is this foolishness going to be over?"

To which I responded, "Not much longer," meaning that I was getting close to my departure date, but I'm sure he thought I meant things would go back to normal for them soon.

I will either escape or be carted off by men in white coats. Yes, I am headed to crazy town. They're coming to take me away, ha ha.

Chapter 4

I'm enjoying my little vacation. I've managed to get most everything on my list done. My little secret nest egg has grown substantially. I should have enough money to sustain me for at least six to nine months after I put money down on my new condo. Then I can begin filling it with the things that I want to take with me.

I've filed separation papers, and my husband will be served in a few weeks. I found my lawyer through the firm at work, someone we used in the past. She has lived a parallel life and is applauding my courage to go through with actually doing something about my situation. I'm to keep her informed as things progress. I may be starting a movement. Women unite, you are allowed to put yourself first again. If you are unhappy with the life you have, there's hope!

I've found where I want to live. I'm so excited about my condo. It's so neat and orderly. It isn't far from our family subdivision and is gated. I can hardly wait to begin moving in. Everything in there will be mine, all mine. I can do whatever I want, when I want. There will be no one there to judge me or complain about anything.

I am going to be free to live as I want, play music, watch what I want on TV; no condemnation, no interruption, no aggravation, no irritation, no one there to neglect my needs, ignore me, be disappointed in me, put me down, or push me around. Finally, a place on earth where I won't say everything wrong, do everything wrong. Whew! I'm feeling lighter by the minute.

Okay, rant over. Next order of business, start packing.

Fortunately, when a person wants to pack up their life, an uninterested husband comes in handy. After collecting boxes from behind grocery stores and liquor stores, I filled them with just the items I wanted to take with me. Then, I stacked them inside the garage, waiting to be transported. Jake has walked by the wall of boxes, repeatedly. He hasn't asked the first question as to why there are boxes labeled Campbell's Soup and Jim Beam stacked along the wall. I suppose I should have a response ready. Maybe, if he should ask, I'll just tell him it's some of my things. Truth!

My accounts are set up at the bank, I will be putting in my two-week notice come Monday. By the end of the month, I will have transported the last of my things, and Jake will have been served the separation papers.

At the realtor's office, I signed the mortgage papers for my condo and paid the down payment. When she put the keys in my hand, I couldn't stop the tears. I'm not sure if the emotion was from relief or sadness, maybe a little of both.

I've enjoyed taking a few boxes from the garage each day and placing them just where I want in my new place. Everything looks so neat, the towels all match, the dishes are stacked just so, and everything is in my favorite color scheme—beach, sea, and sweet grass. That's blues, tans, and soft greens, all very light and airy. Most of my furniture, what little I have, is wicker with deep cushions.

My furnishings are simple. All I needed was a bed with a nightstand, a sofa, a rocking chair for reading, an end table, and a kitchen table with two chairs. This is the way I like it, uncluttered with lots of room to move around. It's great what you can order online and have delivered right to your front door.

There are only a couple of things left to do. I am going to use every freezer container in the old house to stock up enough food to do the family for quite a while. I also want to write my children a letter to explain why I'm leaving and what they might need to do to have a successful outcome for their life journey.

As for Jake, I'll let the separation papers explain. I know, cold hearted, maybe I'm a coward, avoiding the confrontation. Either way, those chickens will come home to roost eventually, and I will face them when it happens. Or run away, we'll see.

Chapter 5

My new life has begun. I'm out of here. Goodbye to this cruel world. As I backed down the driveway, I gave our suburbia homestead one last look. It looked a little shabby; the yard was given minimal attention the last few years. The husband was too busy, and the teenagers had their own plans. I reminded myself, *you did the best you could with what tools you had.* That sentiment seems to cover my whole life here.

After the short drive across town to my condo, I punched in my code at the gate and watched it slide open with elation. I felt like the most popular girl in school, part of the It crowd. I belong somewhere.

There is a notice in my mailbox:

MINGLE PARTY
SATURDAY NIGHT 8 P.M.
At the Club House
Bring your dancing shoes!

The Club House was in the middle of the complex with the usual weight room, pool, hot tub, banquet room, and kitchen. At the introduction tour, I found it to be spacious and clean. As the realtor had explained to me, it was part of our HOA fee. I imagined the children visiting me, eager to hang out there and my regaining some kind of relationship with them. They might think it's really great or really lame.

As I'm putting my key in the front door, my cell phone chimes. Digging it out of my purse, I see that it's Jake. He can leave me a message. By the time I put my purse down on my sweet little kitchen table, the phone has dinged with the voicemail tone. I'll listen to it later. He obviously didn't say much. Curiosity getting the better of me, I put in my code and put the voicemail on speaker. After a string of curse words, he vowed to make me pay for my betrayal. My first reaction, my stomach lurched. I had to sit down. For just a moment, I thought I was going to lose my breakfast. My body broke out in a sweat. My arms tingled. Am I having a heart attack? I looked around my kitchen. Making four strides to the door, I double locked it and leaned against it. Taking a deep breath, I reason with myself. It was just Jake's reaction at getting served the papers. He would cool down eventually, and it would be old news. I hope.

I remind myself, the condo complex is gated. He doesn't have the code.

Feeling the need to talk to someone, I call my mother.

Her phone goes to her answering machine. She still has a landline. I don't wait for the beep to disconnect.

Realizing my need for a friend, I google local support groups for women.

After surfing through AA and several other acronyms, I find one for recovery at a church not far from me. There was a meeting tomorrow night. I pull out my day planner and jot down the time and address. I think about calling Aunt Millie and decide against it. She doesn't need my troubles and is probably out working in the fields.

Feeling better, I'd like to use my new shower, during which I try not to think of the movie, *Psycho*.

After dressing in khaki capris and a cotton button-up blouse, I decide to take a walk before lunch and clear my mind. Putting my cell in my back pocket, I lock my front door behind me.

I was enjoying the landscaping and the sun shining down softly when I came upon an elderly couple sitting on a bench in the shade of an oak. "Top of the morning to you," said the man. His companion just smiled.

"I don't believe we have had the pleasure of meeting." He rose, extending his hand in greeting.

Don't you just love people of that generation? They are so mannerist and gentile.

I met his handshake firmly, but not too firm. "Ann Cantrell, nice to meet you both."

"We are the Smiths, Carl and Betsy. Would you like to join us on this beautiful day Ms. Cantrell?" He indicated the empty spot at the end of the bench with a wave of his hand.

"Oh, no, thank you. I'm just out for a walk to take in all my new surroundings," I said, making a waving motion toward the condos.

Betsy spoke with a surprising English lilt in her voice, "Then we will be seeing you around. Maybe get to know one another?"

"Yes, I'm sure we will," I replied. As I'm walking away, I feel an excitement about uncovering their backstory. I think I'm really going to like it here.

After arriving back to my condo, I pulled out my cell phone. No new messages. I really should call Jake back. After all, he has been a good provider all these years, and he was engaged when the children were small. He deserves some respect.

I dialed his number with my hands shaking and my mouth gone dry. He answers on the second ring.

"What the hell, Ann!" I could picture the veins in his forehead that bulge out when he's angry.

"Hi, Jake," I answer softly.

"What's going on?" he demands.

"I just couldn't do it anymore, Jake. I was disappearing. I couldn't breathe. I have just the one life, and I didn't like it. It was empty and lonely. I couldn't do anything right. Everything I did for you and the children went unnoticed or was inadequate according to you and them. There's no love there, no hope, no connection with any of you. Surely you noticed by how frustrated and angry I constantly made you that I wasn't what you wanted or needed."

"You should have said something," he said flatly.

"Ha! All those times I pleaded with you for attention, all the tears and begging for you to spend family time with me and children. And not to mention the bedroom! Where did you go? I was always pulling at you to get involved, to be present!" I cried.

"We must be talking a different language, Ann. Sure, I remember you saying a couple of times that it had been a while since we did anything together. I work hard and take care of this family. Haven't I been a good husband and father?" he asked.

"Yes, Jake, you have been those things at one time, but not anymore. I would trade all the money, the house, and the cars for a connection with you and the kids. We aren't close, we haven't been in a long time. I tried to get us back there, but I couldn't do it alone. The things I do and say seem to rub you the wrong way. I'm done with your anger and disapproval. I want peace in my life. I want a life that's not all work and worry. I want to laugh. I want to dance. I want to be happy, to be in a place where I'm welcome and accepted as myself."

"That's just life, Ann. Not everyone gets to be happy all the time. You want too much. I don't know who you are anymore."

"Me either. Bye, Jake." I'm resigned. He will never understand.

He disconnected first, to my relief.

I sat looking at the phone, wondering if he ever really loved me.

Then I look around my tidy kitchen and decide that I was glad I was here and not back there. I'm so glad to have that confrontation over.

Chapter 6

After stocking my refrigerator and pantry with all my favorite foods, I decided to make a trip to the local library and get myself some excellent reading material. Don't you just love getting lost in a great book? Upon entering, the head librarian said good morning, calling me by name. I'm a regular patron.

I whispered, "What's new, Tonya?" I was so glad to see her friendly face.

Over in the children's corner, I could see Mark doing the special reading time. Some of the children were being attentive, while others were rolling around on their assigned cushions.

"We have that book that you requested," said Tonya.

"Great." I had been on a waiting list and was glad it was finally my turn. "I'm going to look through the stacks too," I told her. She nodded her head okay.

I love being surrounded by books, the smell of them and anticipation of reading them. It has always been my escape and remained the one constant of my life. I could always count on a book to take me on an adventure and help to leave my worries behind for a while.

Many of these books, I've read more than once. I grab a Louis L`Amour (I just love a good western) and a Billie Letts. The twists and turns in her books makes them hard to put down.

As I head back to the check-out desk, I notice job postings on the bulletin board. There were several library branches hiring in our area. When Tonya saw me looking at the notices, her eyebrows went up.

"Ann, are you interested in a job?"

"Yes, I'm going to put in my notice at the law firm. I would so enjoy getting to work around books. It would be a refreshing change."

She looked over the notices and picked out the one that would suit me best.

"This one pays the best and would be with some really good people I know at that branch. Put us down as a reference, and you're sure to get it."

Mark, finished with the children's story, came over to the desk. "Hi, Ann, how are you?"

"Fine," I responded. "Well, okay, I guess." Why did I say I'm fine when I'm not?

"She's applying for a library position," said Tonya.

"Well, since I'm here to relieve you at the desk, why don't you two go to the computers and get her done?" he offered.

Tonya and I said in unison, "Okay." We all three laughed, lowly.

It only took a few minutes, and by the end of our visit, I had an appointment for an interview with the main-branch library downtown. I jotted down the time in my day planner.

Thanking them profusely, I left with my books and a spring in my step.

After arriving back to the condominium complex, I spotted my daughter talking to the guard at the gate. I wondered how she had gotten there and how she knew where to find me. Then, I remembered putting down that information in the letter I had left for her.

"Hi, sweetheart." I smiled my best smile at her.

"Mom!" she said, exasperated. "How could you?"

"Hop in the car, Cindy." I ignored her anger, embarrassed for the guard to witness our family drama. "Thank you," I said to him. I hadn't learned his name yet.

"No problem, Ms. Cantrell," he nodded.

Cindy stomped to the passenger side of the car, slung the door open, and plopped into the seat. Slamming the door, she folded her arms with a pout and stared straight ahead.

I wasn't going to cut her any slack. "Skipping school today?"

"You can't do this to me! Since you left, Dad and Brian want me to do everything that you are supposed to do!" she emphasized with her hands in the air.

"Huh, well, how about that?" I hadn't considered that happening. "What did you say to them?"

"I told them no way I was going to become you."

"Ouch!" I cried.

"It's not good, Mom! You should see the house. It's a wreck. I had no idea how much you did. Please, please come back. We need you," she whined.

"Look around you." I motioned toward the complex. "Just look how nice it is here. Why would I want to go back to that house when I can have all this?"

"Because we need you. We are your family. You have a responsibility to us." She wasn't swayed.

"Oh, Cindy, I know you can't understand just yet, but I couldn't do it anymore. I wasn't being a good mother by doing everything for you and your brother. For some reason, I couldn't get you to step up and do things for yourselves. You will go off to college next year, and then Brian is just two years behind you. You should be working a part-time job after school or weekends. You should be cooking and cleaning, doing your own laundry. You know nothing of how to take care of yourself. And as for our relationship, you wanted nothing to do with me."

I pulled into the garage, cut the engine, and turned to her. "I want to have what I've seen other parents have with their children—families doing things together, being, well, families. I don't have that with you all." My eyes began to tear.

She looked at me. "But you left, Mom. How can we be a family now?"

"Come in and I'll fix you a sandwich, then take you back to school."

"Just take me back. I'm not hungry." She folded her arms and stared at the floorboard.

"Alright, but I want to talk with you sometime about what kind of family you want for yourself someday. I'm hoping the same thing won't happen to you. I think it's true what they say about teaching people how to treat you. I spoiled all of you by doing too much, thinking that it was how to show you that I loved you. I felt guilt from working throughout your childhood, trying to balance work and family. I'm a little mixed up myself on just how to proceed from here, but I do know that I can't go back. I'd suffocate there, completely disappear. I'm hoping to get into a support group, maybe figure things out. I do love you, Cindy, and I'm here any time you want to talk. I'm really hoping to grow something between us that's even stronger than just a mother-daughter thing. I'd like to get to know you. Maybe we can build on that?"

For the first time in a very long time, Cynthia looked me in the eye. I could see the woman she would become at that moment, strong-willed and soulful. I think she heard me.

"Maybe I could come live with you," she suggested.

I wasn't expecting that. "Um, I don't want to risk going back to the way things were. I don't think that would be a good idea. Do you understand?"

She set her mouth in a thin line and nodded, yes.

When we arrived at the high school, she stepped out of the car and turned back to ask, "What should I do about the mess at the house?"

"Tell the men of the house to step up, don't take any of their excuses." I got out of the car and hugged her. "You can do it, Cindy. Let your stubbornness work for you. You're stronger than me."

She almost smiled, just a little at the corners. "Dad's getting me a car. Says I need to get a job now. Because you left, I need to bring in some money."

I wasn't sure how to respond. "You can come visit me any time."

"Whatever," she responded flatly with a shrug.

I watched her walk into the building, saying a little prayer of protection over her.

With a call from Jake and a visit from Cindy, that's two down, one to go.

In thinking about Brian, I wonder if Jake is reminding him to shower. Sometimes he just falls into bed unless someone nudges him to pay attention to his hygiene.

I blow out the breath I found myself holding. I need to talk to someone. The support group is tomorrow. Maybe I can get some answers there.

Chapter 7

Dressing casually–denim jeans, cotton blouse, and tennis shoes–I head to the church where the support group meeting is being held. This particular group meeting is for people in recovery from family experiences like divorce and grief. I don't know if it's a good fit for me. I only know that I should try to figure some things out if I'm to help my children cope with the changes I have dumped on them. This will be my first time in a group like this. The most similar experience I've had would be when Jake and I had counseling before we married. It was one on one with our pastor, not exactly soul baring stuff.

Upon entering the building, I'm assailed with old church smell, something between crayons and worn hymnals. Following the Support Group construction paper signs taped to the walls, I find the room for the meeting. Folding chairs are arranged in a circle in the middle of the room. An old piano is positioned on one wall with the American flag on one side and the Christian flag on the other. More folding chairs are grouped next to the piano with Bibles stacked on them.

Some people had already arrived and were talking softly to each other when I entered.

One of them was Betsy Smith, the elderly lady I met with her husband, Carl, when walking around the condominium complex.

"Hi," she offered with a little wave of her hand. "Ann is your name, right?"

Her accent was gone.

"Oh, I thought you were British," I said, taking an empty seat to her left.

"Nah," she laughed, "I just like messing with people."

I wasn't sure how to respond to that. I looked around the group and noticed the vast age differences. Two of the women looked like teenagers and one looked like she could possibly be their mother. There was a couple in their thirties. I could tell they were a couple because they were arguing about something to do with him not listening to something she had said.

The rest of the group consisted of the elderly (not British) Betsy and a man about my age who looked like life had deflated him.

The lady who looked like the mom of the teens spoke.

"Let's get started. Let's go around the room and introduce ourselves and tell a little bit about why we are here and what we hope to accomplish in this support group. I'll start. My name is Leslie, and my daughters Lee and Lola are experiencing grief at the loss of my husband and their Dad." As one of the daughters rolled her eyes and the other stared at the floor, Leslie put her hand up and said, "He didn't die." Her laugh and demeanor indicated that she wished that were the case. "He left for greener pastures. We started a support group to air grievances and try to understand that people do things like this, and it isn't anyone's fault." She looked over at her girls as she said the last part. Both girls looked very uncomfortable.

She then looked to the couple for their introduction.

"We're Jane and Tyler," the woman responded. "We are here to try and save what's left of our marriage after an incident of . . . infidelity." Her voice got so low at the end that I could barely hear her. Tyler shifted in his seat. I could tell he wanted to be anywhere else. But to his credit, he nodded at his wife as if to say, *I'm in.*

The man of my generation who was alone spoke next.

"Rob is my name. I'm grieving for my wife, Rene. She passed away three months ago, and I'm having a little trouble moving on." He looked around the room with heartache etched in his face and leaking out of his eyes.

I wanted to wrap him in a bear hug.

It was my turn, and I felt like I had no excuse to be there.

"Ann here," I stammered. "Well, I feel like a heel. I have left my family to start a new life. I, um, it was, the, well, our home was, well." I sat up straighter and fortified myself.

"My family had no use for me anymore." I looked over at the abandoned mother and her daughters. "I was disappearing. I wanted a new beginning, and I'm making it happen. I guess I'm here to figure out how I can help my children understand and accept what I've done." As lame as all that sounded, no one seemed to be judging me. They all just looked curious.

It was Betsy's turn. "I'm here for the coffee and gossip." She cackled. "Nah, I'm here because Carl has cancer, and I'm pissed off. This is supposed to be our time. You work your whole life for retirement and to have a little peace, just to find out that one of you won't make it through the year. It's horrific watching what's happening to him!" Her anger erupted.

Leslie uncrossed her legs and put her briefcase on her lap. Apparently, she is the head of the support group.

"Thank you, everyone, for sharing," she said. "It sounds like we are going to have some very interesting discussions. First off, I want to express that I'm qualified to handle grief and life-changing counseling, but for you, Jane and Tyler, I feel that a counselor who deals specifically with marriage would be a better fit for you. That way, you would get the in-depth repair you need." She shrugged. "If you wish to stay, I will give it my best effort."

She produced a business card from her briefcase and handed it to Tyler. "If you wish to call him, this is a colleague who specializes in specific situations such as yours."

The husband got up first, taking the business card, and his wife trailed behind him. She stopped at the door and looked back. "Good luck, everybody." She gave a little wave and started down the hall, following her sorrows.

"Since this is our first meeting," continued Leslie, clearing her throat. "I have some reading material for you, Rob, and for you, Betsy. There's information on dealing with a loved one who is battling cancer and grief." She rose as she produced from her briefcase a pamphlet for Rob and two for Betsy.

"As for you, Ann," she shrugged her shoulders, "I'm not quite sure what to do to help you with starting a new life. Just take it one day at a time, I guess, is the best advice I can give."

They were all staring at me, waiting for a response. "I think I just need to talk it out. To see what others think about my decision and how to handle the fallout."

"You go, girl!" Betsy shouted. "Don't let them take you down. You're young yet. There's plenty of time. Kick up your heels. Make your life what you want it to be. You just get one go-around, so make it count." She punched the air for effect.

"While I love and appreciate your enthusiasm, Betsy," remarked Leslie, "I do have concerns about her children and what they are dealing with at home and school now that their mom has left. What is the family dynamic like for them now? How are they to recover from these changes?" She looked at her daughters on each side of her.

I had the feeling that she was talking more about them than my children.

The rest of the meeting consisted of Rob telling us about the wonder of his wife and how he was afraid of losing his memories of her if he let go of his grief. Leslie gave him some suggestions on how to keep her memory alive while learning to readjust his life in moving forward without her. She also gave her daughters some information about accepting that their non-present father was in no way anyone's fault, and to blame themselves would only be self-destructive and anti-productive. When it became Betsy's turn, Leslie assured her that it was alright to be angry, expected even, but to not let it ruin what time she had left with her husband, Carl. Then she turned to me.

"I think you know what you need to do," she said. "Just keep loving them, make them as much a part of your life as you can without returning to the dynamic from before."

"Thank you, Leslie," I responded. "You make it sound so easy." I truly was grateful. After all, here I was doing basically the same thing her husband had done to their family except for leaving with someone else, a double betrayal.

"Would you like to go get some coffee?" Betsy asked me.

"Sure," I answered with relief that the meeting was over and would probably be my last one.

After thanking Leslie again and wishing the girls and sad Rob well, Betsy and I settled in my car. "Where to?" I asked her.

"I didn't really want coffee, just out of there," she said, pointing toward the church. "Let's go shopping. We could go get something to wear to the social at the Club House tomorrow night. I was going to get Carl to pick me up after the meeting, but I'll text him that you and I are running an errand. He will be relieved. He doesn't like to stray too far from the facilities these days, if you know what I mean." She typed out a text on her cell phone and hit send. "There, done."

"I understand, chemo can be so awful." I sympathized.

Betsy and I were both quiet as we drove down Main Street toward the mall.

"Dillard's or Belk's?" I asked.

"Kmart is more my speed," she answered, looking at me with a stiff turn of her body.

"I heard they were closing."

"Yes, they will be soon." She shook her head.

"Alrighty then, Kmart it is," I responded.

We traveled in silence through the Friday traffic for several minutes until we reached the parking lot, and I cut the engine.

"I almost did what you are doing," Betsy said in a small voice. "But I chickened out. It wasn't that my marriage was bad, it just wasn't going anywhere anymore." She motioned with her hands. "I can't quite explain it right." She let out a heavy sigh.

"You remember that show, *Golden Girls?*" she asked.

"Yes, I love that show," I answered.

"Well," she continued, "one of the characters, named Blanche, she once described a mood where she wasn't happy but wasn't sad. She was confused about exactly what she was feeling. She called it magenta. You know, like the color, not pink, but not quite purple or red. Magenta." She folded her hands in her lap. "I think that's what you are experiencing. Like you don't know exactly what your role is now, where you belong, or where your life is going."

"Magenta, huh? You might have something there."

"I know without a doubt where mine is going." She nodded her head.

"I'm going to buy a hot pink dress to dance in tomorrow night." She laughed. "Anything but black, I refuse to wear black until I just have to."

"Maybe we can find something in magenta for me. Betsy, I think this is the beginning of a beautiful friendship." I linked arms with her.

We entered the store, high-stepping and laughing. The people at Kmart just smiled back at us as we acted like silly teenagers finding each other a new dress for the party.

Betsy settled on a red silk blouse and some gray slacks. I found an A-line green dress I liked that would complement my auburn hair. Magenta was not to be found at Kmart.

Chapter 8

Before I could get my Saturday morning cup of coffee, my phone was ringing. The caller ID showed it to be Brian.

"Hello, sweetheart." I answered with as much enthusiasm as my morning fog brain would allow.

"Mom," he said, stiffly. "Dad said I had to call you sometime."

"Would you like to meet today and let me buy you lunch?" I asked, hopefully.

"Nah, I got a game. Dad might be there." He waited.

"Well, maybe I can take you to lunch tomorrow after church," I suggested.

"Um, awkward, Mom, are you still gonna show your face at church? You've abandoned your family. That's a bad thing, right?" His voice was shaking.

"I'm sorry, baby, I can only imagine how hard all this must be for you. That's why I want to see you face to face and explain further. Didn't my letter help you understand at all?" I ask.

"I tore it up!" he cried.

"Oh, well. Um, what are you doing right now? I'll come pick you up and we'll talk".

"'Kay," he answered softly, engulfing a sob.

"Be there in a flash. It's going to be okay," I assured him.

"Yeah, sure," he responded sarcastically and hung up.

After gulping down a cup of coffee, I prepared another to take with me for the drive to pick up Brian. My mind was organizing my side of the argument as I negotiated the traffic to the house. Then it occurred to me— just love him and be understanding—like God was talking to me, saying, *Be calm, Ann, just be receptive to your son.*

After turning onto the street, I spy Brian waiting just inside the garage. The condition of the house is shocking. No one is mowing the lawn, and all the landscaping is full of weeds. Maybe I did make some difference here.

As I pull into the driveway, Brian slides into the passenger seat. "Let's go before Dad sees you."

Without a word, I reverse and head down the street. I look over at Brian and am amazed at how different he looks. His hands seem more muscular with long fingers. Gone is the baby fat that showed a full face. His usually floppy, brown hair was close shorn. He was becoming a chiseled man. Could it be that his eyes have become more blue than hazel?

"What?" he asked, irritated at my staring.

"It's like you've become a man overnight," I said with wonder.

He stared back at me. Then a look came over his face as if he was seeing me for the first time. "You look different, too, Mom. Brighter, maybe. Is this what leaving us did for you? Made you look happier?"

"I hadn't thought about it much—my looks, that is—since I've been on my own, but yes, I guess leaving all that stress behind would make a person look different," I answer cautiously.

He nodded and turned his head to stare out of the side window.

I pulled into Cracker Barrel and put the car in park. "Let's have some breakfast. I'm starving."

"Sure, it's just that Coach tells us not to fill up on sweets before a game. So, I need to have protein, eggs, and a lot of carbs," he explained.

"I'm impressed, Brian, I didn't know that you were so informed about nutrition."

"There's a lot you don't know about me, Mom." He was so angry and hurt.

"Well, maybe we should get to know each other better," I replied, trying to sound upbeat.

Over our plates full of steak and eggs, Brian and I hashed out what we wanted from each other and why I made the decision to start a new life. Surprisingly, he was glad for me and hoped to do the same for himself. He had the same disconnect with his father and sister. He was disappointed with his family. News to me—he has a girlfriend, Becky. All his spare time from soccer or school is now being spent at her house. I've got to say, it's brilliant that he found another family to feed him and fuss over him. I expressed my excitement about the girlfriend, asking to meet her. He reluctantly agreed, maybe someday.

I did caution him that he needed to learn to be more responsible for himself and not give up on his dad and home so quickly. He responded that I had no room to judge. I could hardly argue with that.

On the way back to drop him off, he had me stop at the end of the street.

"I'll walk from here, Mom. Thanks for breakfast and the talk," he said sincerely.

"I'm so proud of you. Let's do this again, make it our Saturday morning thing?" I asked hopefully.

"Maybe." He shrugged.

I stayed parked at the curb until I saw him walk up to the house and go inside. I pulled away slowly, taking one more look at the neglect of the yard. Part of me wanted to stomp up there and rev up the lawnmower to get it all back into a respectable condition. Nope, not my problem anymore. I chose instead to crank up the radio. Boston was playing "More Than a Feeling." I sang at the top of my lungs. "I see my MaryAnn walking away . . . A . . . A . . ."

I have a party to go to tonight and a job interview next week. Brian and Cindy seem to have forgiven me. Life is good. But even as I'm counting my blessings, something in the back of my mind is nagging at me. What was it Brian said that made my knee jerk? Oh, yeah, it was about church. Tomorrow is Sunday and I can't go back to my church . . . Can I?

Oh, well, I'll ask someone at the party about where they go. Maybe I'll get a new church too. After all, God is everywhere.

I spent the rest of the day immersed in a book. Louis and I were hanging out at the campfire listening to a posse approaching when my doorbell rang.

It was Betsy.

"Hey, girl, come on in," I said as I opened the door.

"Ann, I have a favor to ask, por favor," she asked with a Spanish accent.

"Como estas?" I ask, dusting off my high school Spanish. She looked puzzled at me.

"How are you?" I translated.

"Great . . . Carl is having a good day, and I think he will be able to come to the party tonight." She put her hands to her face in gesture of relief. "Thing is, I can't do a thing with my hair, and I wondered if you knew of a good hairdresser or had some ideas in that department."

"Not really. My hair is sort of wash and go. Other than a little blow drying and hair spray, I don't do much with mine. I was blessed with some natural curl." I shrugged.

"Well, maybe you could do that with mine," she suggested. "It's really hard to hold my arms up for that long of a time, and I'm already pretty exhausted what with stepping and fetching for Carl all day."

"I tell you what. Let's try it, and if it doesn't come out like you want, no harm, no foul. We'll go where I get my hair cut. They take walk-ins." I smiled at her.

"You got a deal." She clapped her hands together.

Sticking her head under my faucet proved to be challenging, but we got her shampooed and conditioned. I combed her long silver hair out and put a dry towel around her shoulders.

"Let's have a cup of tea and let it air dry for a few minutes before we use the blow dryer. I'd like to learn about some of the other condo residents," I suggested.

"Throw in some cookies and I'll tell all." She giggled.

Betsy filled me in on all the colorful characters in our complex. Many were former professionals, lawyers, doctors, and such. Most were retired, some were widows or widowers. Some were folks who were downsizing after finding themselves as empty nesters. I seemed to be on the younger end of the age demographic. One helpful thing I learned is our daytime guard is named Ben, and our evening guard is named Jim.

After drying her hair with a round brush, soft curls started to take shape. Because of the length, it took a while to get it completely dry.

"How about we go with an updo?" I suggest.

"I'm in your hands," she answered.

After a few attempts with bobby pins and some hair spray, it was coming together. One final spray and voile, Cinderella was ready for the ball.

"Thanks, Ann, it looks great. I found a scarf that matches my slacks and blouse. I'm going to look like a million bucks tonight." She winked at me.

As she bounded out the door, she waved and said, "Tootles, thanks for everything, see you tonight!"

I checked my phone for the time. Guess I should hit the shower and start getting myself ready. The party starts in a couple of hours.

Chapter 9

With my shower completed and my makeup and hair done, I wiggled into my new green dress and my favorite leather pumps. With one last check in the mirror, I decided that I didn't look too bad. My new dress made me feel just a hint of confidence and, dare I think it, somewhat attractive. It's a shame that there's no one to attract. I wouldn't want the baggage that comes with a relationship anyway. So, I'm looking good for me and that's okay.

After the short stroll from my condo to the club house, I entered through the double doors. The room was quiet. Tables for dinning were arranged along the walls on each side of the room with the buffet tables laden with food on the wall that adjoins the kitchen. Plants and splashes of lighting made the room look colorful. The ceiling was decorated with twinkle lights, and candle flames were dancing on the tables. The only thing missing was people.

The side doors to the pool opened, and several couples entered the room, talking with each other.

"Can you believe her? What a character," said a lady in a flower print dress.

"I know," agreed her companion in his dapper suit. "She's always up to something."

Betsy entered wearing a blanket. Her fashionable updo was soaked and plastered to her head.

"Oh, no, Betsy. What happened?" I asked, my hand covering my shocked face.

Betsy laughed. "Oh, not much, just got a little too close to the edge of the pool. Will you keep an eye on my Carl while I get into something less uncomfortable, please?" Off she went.

"Of course," I called after her.

Carl was just a few feet away, moving at a slow pace. The bright, jolly face I remembered from our first meeting was downcast and ashen. His cancer treatments had taken quite a toll on his appearance.

"Let's sit at our table," he motioned toward the back of the room.

"Are you hungry? May I bring you a plate?" I offered.

"Sure, just a little for me," he answered. "Keep it on the bland side. Spicy food is not very friendly to me these days." He patted his stomach and took a seat.

Making my way back to the food table, I found myself in a line of smiling faces. Everyone seemed friendly but didn't say anything to me. I'm a stranger to them.

I got chicken, mashed potatoes, green beans, and a roll for Carl and the steak, potatoes, and a salad for myself. Balancing the plates, I made my way back to our table.

"Oh, nice, thank you." Carl seemed pleased with his food choices.

"What exactly happened out there with our Betsy?" I asked as I took a bite.

"She loves to dance. As we were waltzing by the pool, she asked me to dip her. Well, I tried." He lifted both arms. "I just don't have the strength I once did and plop! Down she went into the water. Yes, not the kind of dip we had in mind." He shook his head and grinned. "Never a dull moment with Betsy."

We were both laughing as Betsy swept into the room. She made her way to the buffet line wearing a burgundy dress with a floral scarf across her shoulders. Her long silver hair was pulled back in a chignon and fastened with a silver comb. She looked fabulous.

Carl leaned in and said, "Ann, Betsy puts on a good front. She's going to need someone very soon. We don't know how much longer I may have. I'd like to think that she won't be completely alone in making decisions. I think God sent you just in time. She seems to really enjoy your company and is so uplifted when she comes home from one of your visits. Quickly, before she gets to the table . . . I know you have a lot going on, but do you think you could stand by her when . . . well, when I'm no more?"

I looked into his imploring eyes. Who could say no? "Of course. I just hope I can keep up with her," I answered as Betsy glided into her seat.

Carl took Betsy's hand and kissed it. "So glad you could finally join us, my little mermaid. You look beautiful!"

Betsy beamed at him. "Nothing like a nice swim to start your evening." She looked over at me. "Ann, don't you look nice."

I couldn't get a response past the lump in my throat. Their kindness and affection toward each other made me tearful. I pushed my plate away. I had lost my appetite. I noticed Carl had been pushing his food around and hardly eaten any of it.

"Would you mind, my darling, if I asked Ann to dance?" he asked Betsy.

"I think that's a fine idea. You kids go on. I'm going to give this piece of chicken something to cluck about," she answered with big eyes. Pain is hard to hide.

As Carl took my hand, the music changed to Glenn Miller's "String of Pearls."

Carl slowly waltzed me around the open floor, his hand placed perfectly in the center of my back. I surprised myself that I could follow his movements. It was as if we were floating on air.

Just as the song ended, Betsy tapped me on the shoulder and stepped into her man's embrace. I watched in awe. The two became one as Carl led her around the room to the song, "Last Date."

I was witnessing one more example of why they were called the Greatest Generation. Even the way they danced back then had such class.

I felt a sharp stab of pain in my chest. I recognized it immediately—loneliness, the ache of something missing. If confused moments were magenta, this one was a dark blue.

I said my goodnights, making an excuse of not feeling well, leaving Betsy with a puzzled look on her face.

As I slid out the door, I looked back at the couple that had become a big part of my life. Exhausted from their dance, they were talking closely at the candle-lit table. No doubt Betsy was working on a good and bright memory that she would need for a darker time to come.

And here I am, going home to my lovely, empty condo. I can feel the doubts start to creep in. Just like when the children were pressuring me to do something, and I struggled with deciding. I was their sole compass to right and wrong, safe and dangerous, and the inevitable outcome of my making the wrong choice, no matter what. My husband, ever the good guy, left it to me.

Why am I suddenly feeling lonely? It must be because of seeing Carl and Betsy's connection and the way they are with each other. Did Jake and I ever have that? Our relationship seemed to be one goal after another, like a check list. Job, check; house, check; kids, check; work harder for more money for kids and house, check. Somewhere in there, we lost the reason for work, home, and kids . . . love.

Maybe tomorrow will be better. Then, I remember it's Sunday. Maybe I'll just rest like the Lord did on the seventh day.

Turning the key at my condo and pushing the door open, I call out, "Honey, I'm home." My voice echoes in the emptiness.

Chapter 10

Waking on Sunday morning, my eyes were stuck together. I had fallen into bed without removing the extra makeup for the party. Now I remember why I don't wear a lot of paint on my face.

Clicking the TV on, I look through the fridge for something to stop my growling stomach just as my cell phone chimes.

"Good morning," I try a cheerful greeting.

"Ann?" said Jake, like it's a question. "Would you like to go to church with us this morning and maybe catch some lunch after?"

My mouth says, "Sure," before my brain could argue. I should never answer the phone before coffee in the morning. It may have been deeper than that. Like the lonely stab of pain from the night before, but my brain isn't firing on all cylinders. So, it looks like I am spending the day with my family. What could go wrong with that?

"Would you like to drive to the house, or should we pick you up?" asked Jake very nonchalantly.

"I'll drive." I answer just a little too quickly. I really am not ready for them to all be here at my sanctuary.

"Okay, see you in about an hour?" he asked.

Do I hear hope, regret, or concern in his voice? Nah, can't be. Let's not get ahead of ourselves.

"See you then," I responded. *Oh, my goodness, what time is it?*

I see from my microwave clock that it is 8:30 a.m. I prepare a cup of coffee and run to my closet to stare at my wardrobe. Grabbing my dress from last year's Easter, a solid tea-length yellow eyelet lace number, I get the shower started to heat up. After retrieving my coffee, I jump into the shower with it, because I can do things like that now without criticism. That helps me to remember the precarious situation I may be driving into.

After giving my hair a few more moments with the blow dryer, I grab my purse, keys, and cell phone and head out to meet the family.

They are all in Jake's car and waiting for me when I pull into the driveway. I notice that someone has mowed the yard and pulled weeds from the landscaping. The house looks like it's breathing again.

I slide into the front passenger seat, just like so many times before.

"Hi," Jake smiles at me. "I'm so glad you're going with us."

"Thanks for inviting me. I wasn't real sure what I was going to do with my day." I smile back. In the back of my mind, I'm thinking, *Be careful, don't get lured into a trap.*

I turn and look at the children in the back seat. They both stare at me, big eyed.

Brian breaks the ice. "Hi, Mom, where do you think we should have lunch?"

"How about we go to Shoney's and do the buffet? What do you think?" I asked.

"Nothing with a sneeze guard, please?" responded Cynthia.

"You could order off the menu," Jake interjected. Wow, look at him, coming up with a solution.

The rest of the drive to church was quiet. The children sat with us during the service of worship singing, sermon, and prayer. Church members were friendly, but I could tell from some of the curious stares that word was out about my fleeing the scene of the crime.

We made our way back to Jake's car just as one of the single, younger-than-myself women beckoned him over for a chat. He listened intently while she twisted this way and that, curling her long blonde hair on the end of her finger. As the conversation ended, she walked away swaying her hips and gave him a backward look across her shoulder that would melt butter.

Jake put his hands in his pockets and studied the ground for a moment before making his way to the car. His face was flushed a crimson red. I slipped into the back seat with Cynthia. Sensing a change in the atmosphere, my place was no longer next to my husband. Shouldn't I be feeling jealously, anger, something?

Jake slid into the driver's seat and closed the door. He turned to look back at me.

"I'm sorry you had to see that. She's been after me since word got out that we are separated. I'm not sure how to handle it. But believe me, there's nothing between us. I still consider myself a married man," he explained. "Now, who's hungry? I know I am. I haven't eaten today."

He looked at me deeply, searching my face. So deeply that I felt a little discomfort.

Does he still love me? I'm not sure how to react to any of this.

The drive to the restaurant was quite uncomfortable. Cindy and Brian were wordless with heads bent toward the illumination of their phones. Jake gave me repeated looks in the rear-view mirror. He had big question marks in his eyes.

He is still quite handsome. I can see why someone would flirt with him without knowing the day-to-day Jake. He's a catch, but I know the truth of it all. As soon as he has her, she will disappear with the exception of his corrections and admonishments.

I began to stare straight back at him as if to say, *I'm not afraid of you. You cannot manipulate me anymore.* I shouldn't have agreed to join them today. If it weren't for Cindy and Brian, I would bolt.

With the exception of Jake insisting on a table and rejecting a booth, our meal was uneventful. I wonder why Jake preferred a table but didn't dare ask. I do remember a time when we would get a booth and sit on the same side, his arm around the back and his body turned toward me while he excitedly talked about our future and flirted with me.

During our meal, Brian spoke about his coach and the soccer team, Cindy talked about graduation and college applications, and Jake talked about the next job his company would be bidding on.

I told them about my job interview at the library next week, which made them all quiet again. I guess it was the feeling that I was truly moving on with my life, another change.

Riding back to the house, Jake invited me in for coffee. I hesitated but answered yes after Cindy asked if I'd look over her college brochures and help her make a decision as to what would be best for her.

Jake unlocked the door. Cindy and Brian bounded up the stairs to their rooms. The house smelled like someone had burned bacon that morning. There was a memory in every corner of the house. I froze in the entryway. Jake brushed past me, removing his suit jacket and loosening his tie.

Standing within inches of my face, he looked deeply into my eyes.

"What happened to us, Ann?" he asked tenderly.

"I'm not sure how you think of it, but I think we became something other than a couple." I spoke slowly, measuring each word. "Maybe you became so entrenched in your work and I became the one responsible for the home and the children, resulting in us growing apart." I waited for a response. He looked at the floor, thinking it over.

I continued. "You were very critical of me, and I was neglected romantically as your partner in this family. My life had become nothing but work and frustration. I poured myself into this house and the children, not doing them any favors by letting things slide and not getting any support from you when it came to discipline or training. I'm standing here trying to explain myself and feel that I'm failing to get you to understand. I feel that I have no hope of you getting what I'm trying to say. My view is that you think you can do no wrong, and I can't do anything right. We have one life, Jake, and I didn't like the one I was living. So, I had to bail on this one and start a new one. Is it possible for you to grasp any of what I'm saying?"

He put his hands in his pockets and heaved a sigh. "You may be right on this one, Ann. But it was not something strong enough for you to abandon us."

Cindy came halfway down the stairs. "Mom, come to my room and we'll go over the brochures and my acceptance letters."

Relief washed over me as I left Jake and followed Cindy to her room. Surprisingly, it was clean. "I tidied up a little while you were talking to Dad," she explained, blushing.

We sat on the edge of her bed and read over each acceptance letter and brochure, narrowing it down to two, East Tennessee State University and Carson Newman University. She admitted that she was leaning more toward ETSU because some of her close friends were going there, and she could still live at home. She wants to be a nurse. It's amazing.

In just a few weeks, my children had matured, just as I had hoped they would. I felt conflicted. I was proud of their growth but sad that it took my stepping out of their lives for that to happen. I must look forward, not back, thinking of the relationship we can have now and in the future.

"I'm so proud of you, Cindy!" I grabbed her in a hug. "You are going to make a terrific nurse. What made you choose the healthcare field?"

She slowly pulled away from our hug and looked at me, puzzled. "Mom!"

Oh no, I've woken the old Cindy, poked the bear. I started to say sorry and caught myself. New me, new me, don't slip back into old me.

She saw me cringe and softened. "I thought I had told you. I've wanted to be a nurse since I can remember. Maybe I didn't tell you." She looked at me with big eyes.

"It's okay, sweetie." I patted her arm. "We are all finding our way," I assured her.

She relaxed her shoulders and smiled.

"One thing, Mom." She pulled away and leaned against her headboard. "What about Brian? Who's going to take care of him and Dad? I'll be swamped with classes and won't even be able to concentrate for worrying about them." She shook her head.

Am I being manipulated? Looking at her innocence expression, I'm taken back to when she was five and tried to convince me that kindergarten was just so much nonsense and she didn't need to start school until she was at least nine or ten.

"Really working the guilt muscle aren't you?" I gave her a sideways grin. "You know, your dad is a grown man. Brian can still come to me if he needs my help."

"It was worth a try." She shrugged. "Still, this is where you belong, with your family. What's the end game here, Mom, divorce? I think you're being awfully selfish." She folded her arms and gave me a level stare.

"Et tu, Brutus?" I suddenly felt exhausted. I need to go home before Brian gets his turn at me. They just don't get it and probably never will.

I pulled myself to a full stand and looked down at her. "Life flies by, Cindy, so fast. I was young once, full of dreams and aspirations. Even with all my compromises on those dreams, I could have been happy if I'd had a loving companion and obedient, appreciative children." I was getting weary with the repetition of explaining myself. "All three of you need to take some responsibility in my leaving, too." There, I'm not taking it anymore. This could have been a day of bonding, but it turned into a day of straightening me out instead.

I left Cindy's room and started down the stairs. Brian was waiting for me at the bottom of the stairs.

"Hey, Mom. What's it going to be? Are you moving back home?" He gave me a hateful stare. Apparently, the three of them had a plan for this day. Operation: Get Mom Back Home.

I didn't reply. I hugged him, but he stood stiff and unyielding. I scooted out the door and headed for my car. I've disappointed them again.

Jake came running to the side of my car as I started the engine. "Why are you leaving? I thought we were going to have coffee?"

I shook my head no. I didn't need any more convincing that I needed to get away from them.

Taking a deep breath, I backed slowly out of the driveway and turned for home, back to my haven of solitude.

Chapter 11

After a fitful night of sleeping off and on, I was ready to go to the law office and put in my two-week notice. Fortunately, they were expecting me to do just that. When I arrived, my exit paperwork was ready and plans for a replacement were already in the works. I didn't mind the efficiency, but it felt a little weird to not have any farewell ceremony, bon voyage celebration, something. The son of my former boss did wish me well.

So, with a cardboard box of the few personal items from my desk, I walked out, unemployed and free as a bird. It was such a strong feeling that I could almost taste the emptiness. Were all those years wasted? One thing you can't get back is time.

As I pulled out into traffic to make my way home, I tried not to think back on my years at the firm, but as we all know, the more you try to not think of something, the harder it pushes into your thoughts.

My cell phone chimed. I could see it was Betsy calling. I pulled off the road into a Mexican restaurant parking lot just in time to answer her call.

"Hola, mi amiga!"

"Ann?" she asked. "Is that you?"

"Oh, sorry, I was attempting to be cute," I replied.

"You didn't sound like yourself. But it could be my hearing. What are you up to today?" She sounded hopeful.

"I'm free as you can be . . . just quit my job at the law firm and I'm ready for adventure," I answered, determined to sound cheerful.

"Let's do lunch, my treat considering you no longer have a job." She chuckled. "The caregivers are here with Carl for the next couple of hours, doing his exercises and getting his readings. I'd like to take advantage of the short respite," she said tiredly.

"On my way," I said, clicking my phone off and pulling back into traffic.

Betsy and I chose a downtown cafe for our lunch date. It was a pleasant crowd for a Monday. The diners consisted of men and women in business wear having a power lunch and retirees. That would all change in a few weeks when school would close for summer recess.

We requested outside seating and settled in, sipping our iced tea as we waited for our grilled chicken salads to arrive.

"Okay, Ann. Tell all. What happen with the family yesterday?" Betsy insisted.

"It was a set up. They didn't really want to spend the day with me. It was more that they wanted to convince me that I needed to return to my gerbil wheel of a life." I shrugged.

"That's too bad. I hate that for you." She shook her head. "So, where does that leave you with your marriage and the children?"

"I'm not sure." I sat my tea glass down and dried my hands on my napkin. "I suppose it's the same as before, separated from Jake and still trying to get some kind of relationship with Brian and Cindy." I held my open hands up in surrender.

"Well, you have that job interview on Wednesday, hopefully that will go well," she said with the enthusiasm of a cheerleader.

"My only worry with that is that the girl whose position I'm filling is on maternity leave. What happens when she decides to come back?" I frowned.

Betsy folded her arms and said, "My saintly mother would say to not borrow trouble and leave that worry for another day." She nodded her head for emphasis.

"You're right. I'm just expecting bad things to happen, probably because of my guilt over leaving Jake and the kids. Jake thinks that my feeling neglected by him and unappreciated by the children isn't enough reason for me to leave. What do you think about that?" I asked.

"Well," she said just as the salads arrived.

We both thanked the waiter and Betsy prayed over our food. "Thank you, God, for the time I've had with Carl. Give him a good day. Help Ann with her situation and her family to understand. Amen."

"Thank you, Betsy. I must sound like a real whinny hinny with all you have to deal with right now. Why do you put up with me?" I asked.

"I think you are right in wanting a life worth living. But I do think you need to figure things out before you completely end your marriage," she suggested. "When I'm confused about things, I take a little walk or go window shopping. Getting away from the situation for a little while helps me to get a different perspective. You have been such a blessing to me, and I wish you only happiness and peace."

"Right back at you, chick!" I laughed.

After our lunch, I kept going over in my mind what she had said about getting away. My mind went back to a simpler time and the happiest of my childhood. What if I contacted Aunt Millie and had a few days back on the farm? Would that help me to work out the why and what of my decisions?

The more I thought about it, the more I liked the idea.

Aunt Millicent Carson, sister to my father, had been a widow since her husband passed away after a tractor accident in the early 1970s. She had never remarried and raised her two children, my cousins Aaron and Emily, on her own. Since becoming adults, they had both moved off to other states. Aaron was a career Navy man with his own family in Virginia, and Emily had become a schoolteacher in Atlanta. She never married. We had our suspicions as to why, but no one in the family had ever mentioned it out loud, probably because of my father being a minister and such a stoic one at that.

When I think of my aunt, I remember her laughter, a complete belly laugh. She seemed to be constantly in movement. If she wasn't directing her field hands, she was cooking or cleaning. Even when she would be sitting in the evening on the front porch after a long workday, she would be swinging or tapping her foot.

The summer visits continued with her two grandchildren after they became school age. I, however, had not seen her since a family reunion several years ago.

When I tried to share my favorite childhood memories with my children, they made a face and let me know they would never be interested in spending that time away from their friends. They preferred summer camp and mission trips with the church's youth group. I understood, but it made me sad for them to miss out on something that I felt had molded me into having a strong work ethic and exercising my creative muscles. When you are that far away in the country, you make your own fun. There were no electronics or immediate entertainment, just the occasional hayride or church event that brought the community together.

I should call her and see if she minds my visiting for a few days. Maybe this weekend I could drive to the farm. If things aren't weird by my being there, I might stay a couple of days. It might help me remember who I was before Jake and the children.

Chapter 12

After a restless and sleepless night, I made my way to check my mailbox. It was overstuffed with all my forwarded mail. Among the junk mail was a thick envelope sent as certified mail with a law firm's address in the upper left corner. The entrance guard must have signed the certification card. There was also a letter from my mother. I decided to go with the lesser of two evils and open my mother's letter.

After three lines of catching me up on what was happening with my father and the church, marriages, new members, and deceased folks, she acknowledged my change of living conditions. She is apparently horrified that I have become the main subject in the rumor mill of the church. She asked me to please reconsider because God and my father hate divorce. In closing, she suggested I make myself more available to my husband. I resisted the temptation to tear the letter into little shreds. I'd like Betsy to read it. She likes Shakespearian-type comedies.

The other piece of scary mail turned out to be divorce papers from Jake. I suppose Sunday's attempt to return me to my position triggered this response. He must have been prepared to send it if things didn't go his way. I shouldn't be surprised, but I am a little confused.

It's time for a phone conversation with my lawyer.

After a not-so-quick call to her office, she requested that I send her a copy of the divorce papers to read over. She advised me not to panic.

I had a little trouble with my printer and downloading the papers onto my computer. My hands were shaking. I tried to fight back the tears, but sobs were escaping. It took several tries to complete the file and attach it to an email to my lawyer.

While it was winging its way through the world wide web, I read over the papers, searching for what Jake was wanting. It seemed quite fair. He wanted to keep the house and buy out my half of the ownership. His grounds were irreconcilable differences. As for the children, that were hardly children anymore. He wanted shared custody. It all seemed a little too fair. I think I smell a big fat rat.

Grabbing my cell, I phoned the house. He still had a landline because he needed a fax machine for his business. Anger was starting to take over my initial reaction of shock.

"Hello," answered a sticky sweet female voice, not my daughter's.

"Hello," I respond. "Who is this?"

"Why, sugar, it's Shirley, of course. To whom do I have the pleasure of speaking?" she drawls.

"Shirley, Shirley who?" I demanded.

A vision of the gold-digging blonde from my failed Sunday visit with the family broke through my cloud of confusion. I disconnected the call.

That was mighty fast. A little too fast!

It was all making sense now. How long had this been going on? Why would she be at our house and answering the phone? Unbelievable, Jake! It's all happening so quickly. I shake my head, trying to clear the cobwebs.

There's nothing like being five-alarm irate to make you brave.

I punch in Jake's cell number.

He answers on the third ring.

"Cantrell Construction, Jake Cantrell speaking." He sounds so steady and together. *Big shot* businessman.

My anger fueled me as I demanded, "How long has this thing with Miss Shirley with the hips been going on?"

"Does it matter?" he asks as if he's bored.

"It most definitely does!" I insist.

"Just sign the papers, Ann," he said with that condescending tone he knows I hate.

"How long, Jake?" I demand.

"Well, if you must know, Shirley has always been interested. I reciprocated her attentions when I felt there was nothing for me any longer with you. Which, if you need an exact date, I really don't remember. She has been in the back of my mind for a while. I only acted on it when things became difficult," he stated flatly. "She is everything you're not. An old-fashioned girl who wants to be a homemaker, taking care of her man and the family. It's a refreshing change for me, and it lets you off the hook. Let's face it, Ann, you weren't very good at it anyway."

I was seeing red. "How dare you? You cheat! If I hadn't worked, you wouldn't have been able to build the construction business. You just wait; your little cutie pie in a frilly apron won't be able to keep you happy long. I give it six months before she wonders what she's bought into. You're an ogre, Jake! You are a nit-picking fault finder and horribly disrespectful to women. You neglected me and belittled me every chance you got. Shame on you!" I disconnected the call, hanging up on him. Cell phones are limited when it comes to anger. I miss that satisfying feeling of slamming down the receiver to hang up on someone.

I paced around the condo for a few minutes.

When my cell rang, I let it go to voicemail.

I went to my bedroom and fell face down on the bed, letting my grief take over. I sobbed into my pillow. Why? Why couldn't he love me? What was wrong with me?

Wait a minute. It's not me! It's him. He is an indecent cheat. Period. I will not waste another minute crying over him.

Finding my cell phone on the floor by my bed, I checked my voicemail.

My lawyer advised that I sign the divorce papers and accept the more than adequate offer Jake made for my half of the house.

So, I did.

Then, I felt better.

Then, I called Betsy, telling her everything.

She listened intently without comment. When I had finished all the drama that had been my morning, I asked her, "Why is Jake like this? Did I cause him to be that way?"

Betsy sighed. "I can't explain men to you, Ann. I look at it like this: men are like hallways, and women are like rivers."

"How do you figure that?" I asked.

"Men go through life doing basically one thing at a time. In a hallway there are many doors. The job is the room behind one door. The wife is another door and so on. It's compartmentalized. With women, we are like a river. Everything that has ever happened or will ever happen flows along with us. We carry our jobs, our family, and everything else along with us as we move through our lives. That is why women are so much better at multitasking."

"Wow, that's deep Betsy." I was smiling. "I think you have something there, thank you."

"You are welcome, dear one," she answered. "Sometimes wisdom comes with the wrinkles, and other times you can't find the glasses that are sitting on top of your head."

We both laughed. She had to get back to Carl. I could hear worry in her voice. She is concerned that he isn't doing well.

Looking through my stack of books for a distraction, I picked up the latest in the *Miss Julia* series by Ann Ross. Not only did we share a name, but we also shared the enjoyment of an adventurous woman setting things right in her small corner of the world.

After reading a couple of chapters, I feel fortified.

Making my way to the bedroom, I lay out my outfit for my first day at the library position—white slacks and a turquoise blouse with my matching slipper shoes. I will be comfortable and not too dressy.

As I make my way to the kitchen, I decide to have stir fry and rice for my evening meal. That will sit well on my poor, tragic stomach. I can put this day behind me and look forward to the next.

A thought hit me out of the blue. What if Miss Reason for the Irreconcilable Differences isn't good to Cindy and Brian? Maybe I should call her back and make nice.

Nah, awkward isn't a strong enough word for that scenario. And besides, they aren't defenseless children. Memories of Sunday's visit confirms that to be true.

Therefore, I instruct myself to let it lie, Ann. Just let it lie.

Chapter 13

Wednesday morning came around, just as if the entire world had not changed. After a fitful night of tossing and turning, my head was heavy, and my eyes burned. I had spent the whole night pushing thoughts away. Just when I felt myself starting to drift off in a relief of sleepiness, images of Jake and his flirting floozy started pecking at my brain.

It was so not a good day to have a job interview. There was nothing to help it. I needed to pull myself together.

After my morning ritual of drinking coffee and dressing, I popped some medication for my aching head. There was nothing to numb the pain in my heart. It felt like there was a rock the size of a boulder in my chest, and for some reason, I was having trouble swallowing. Every few minutes, involuntary tears leaked from my eyes. Yes, I was in full heartbreak mode.

In a fog, I gathered my application and references and headed to my car. Realizing that I had forgotten my purse, I turned on my heel and went back inside.

Shaking the cobwebs from my head, I stubbornly refused to give in to how I'm feeling. Not keeping the appointment wasn't an option. I need this job. Okay, maybe not this job but a job.

On my second attempt at leaving, Betsy came bounding up the driveway.

"I'm glad I caught you. Good luck on your interview," she said cheerfully.

She gasped, her expression changing to shock. "Ann, no offense, but you look terrible. Oh, you poor thing. You have circles under your eyes, and it's either a new fashion trend or your blouse is inside out," she said as she touched the exposed seam on my shoulder.

"I suppose I should call them and reschedule," I responded flatly, defeated.

Digging my phone out of my purse, I punched in the numbers provided on the application.

"Good morning, Knox County Library," the operator answered.

"Good morning, may I please speak to the person in charge of job interviews?" I couldn't think of her name to save my life at that moment. Then, I see it on my sticky note attached to the application. "Miss Jacoby."

"One moment please," responded the youthful, cheerful operator.

While I was on hold, Betsy and I made our way back inside. I sat down at the kitchen table. She began to prepare us a cup of coffee.

"Miss Jacoby," answered the voice on my phone. "How may I help you?"

"Good morning, Miss Jacoby. I have an appointment for an interview with you today and am a bit under the weather. Is it possible for me to reschedule?" I cringed, feeling like I was lying to this nice lady.

"Oh, yes, Mrs. Cantrell, we've had a development. I'm just arriving at the office and hadn't gotten the chance to phone you. That position is no longer open. There has been an, um . . . occurrence with the young lady that, well, I can't say much because it's rather personal. The fact is, she will remain one of our employees. I'm sorry, I wish you the best. If another position should open, I'll be sure to contact you."

"Thank you," I responded, perplexed. "What happened with the girl's pregnancy? Is she alright?" I asked.

"Yes, she will be, eventually. Again, I'm sorry," she said.

I disconnected the call, looking at Betsy. Her eyebrows were up. "The job is no longer open. I think the girl they were filling the position for may have lost her baby. How horrible for her."

I groaned, cupping my head between my hands. "What am I to do now? My money will eventually run out. Well, at least until I get a settlement on my half of the house from Jake." I threw my hands up in bewilderment.

"How can I feel sorry for myself when that poor girl may have lost her child?"

"Oh, come on now. This isn't you." Betsy put her hands on her hips. "Where is that girl who had the courage to change her life? Frankly, I'm a little disappointed. I thought you were this go-getter with steely determination. What's to become of us wimps if a little thing like the end of your marriage and the possibility of becoming homeless could take you down?" She made a face at me.

After a pause, we both laughed together.

"I know you're right. I just need time to think." I nodded my head.

"You will figure this out. Now, I've got to scoot home. Carl was looking ashen this morning. His care nurse is taking his vitals, and I want to catch her before she leaves. You're going to be okay. I'll check back in with you later." She gulped down some of her coffee and rinsed the cup out at the sink. "Tootles," she waved over her shoulder as she slid out the door.

What to do, what to do, was all I could think. I secured the door and made my way to my bed. Falling on it, I lay there looking at the ceiling. I could sell my car and take the bus. A picture of lugging groceries on the bus came to mind, and I shook it away. No one would want to buy my old Ford Taurus sedan. It's almost a classic and beige, just a boring get-you-there car. I was going to hand it down to Cindy. A memory came back to me of the face she made when I suggested she could use it for college. She would be getting the VW Cabrio her dad had promised her. Probably a guilt gift.

I could sell my jewelry. Looking at the wedding band and modest diamond ring, I realized how much I had sold myself short in my marriage. I've seen more elaborate rings on women with much fewer financial means. Pulling them off, I rubbed the indentation on my finger, then tossed the rings on the nightstand. Most of my other jewelry was costume or cubic zirconium. I might get a couple of hundred bucks for all of it. It's not quite worth the effort or humiliation of trying to sell it all.

I felt myself drifting off to sleep. The line from *Gone with the Wind* went around in my head: "I won't think about that now. I'll think about that tomorrow. After all, tomorrow's another day."

I woke with a start. The room was completely dark. I could hear thunder far off. My cell phone was buzzing. I had left it on the kitchen table. Before

I could stumble to pick it up, it had gone to voicemail. Blinking, I opened up the app and hit speaker and play.

"Ann, could you come to the hospital ER, please? Carl has taken a turn for the worse, and I could use a friend right now." Betsy asked so softly I could hardly make out her words.

I ran to the bathroom and scrubbed the sleep out of my eyes and brushed my teeth, trying to wake myself up. I changed my rumpled clothes into jeans, a T-shirt, and a hooded jacket.

With my keys, purse, and cell phone in hand, I locked up my condo and ran for the car. She started right up—nothing wrong with this car. She is reliable. It hit me that you are what you drive—ugh!

The rain was coming down in sheets as I arrived at the hospital emergency parking lot.

Grabbing an umbrella from the backseat floorboard, I locked my car and ran for the door. The wind turned my umbrella inside out. I managed to fold it back into place but was soaked by the time I hit the revolving door.

Betsy was standing at the nurse's station talking with a doctor.

"I'm sorry." He was saying as he patted her back.

Just as he turned to start down the hall, Betsy saw me and ran to me, collapsing in my arms. She felt so small and fragile.

"He's gone," she cried. "He's really gone."

I held my friend until she was done crying. I used my T-shirt tail, the only dry thing I had, to dab at her tears, which made her chuckle softly.

"I knew it was coming," she said. "I guess I was in denial that it would really happen."

It was my turn to encourage her. "You can do this. Just one step at a time. I will help you with whatever I can."

She just nodded her head. "Paperwork and phone calls. We'll get started tomorrow."

We made our way to the nurse's station and asked all the questions Betsy needed to ask about what to do next. They would hold Carl's body in the morgue until arrangements were made. She asked to see him so she could say goodbye.

I waited for her by the door, leaning against the wall and staring at the pattern on the floor.

When she was ready, I held Betsy's arm and led her to my car. It was just beginning to become daylight; everything looked gray. The storm had subsided into a fine mist.

When we arrived at the condominiums, I suggested she stay with me. I wasn't sure how things had been left at her place and didn't want her walking back in there alone.

After a cup of sleepy time tea, Betsy put on my softest pajamas. I tucked her into my bed for some much-needed rest. As I made myself a nest on the sofa, I said a prayer for Betsy and my children. *God, give me guidance to navigate all these changes.*

It was mid-afternoon when we woke. Betsy looked as wrung out as I felt. We did manage to make a few phone calls. Planning a funeral would be a new experience for me.

Betsy seemed calm and began to come around to her old self. She had but one goal, to honor her husband and his memory. My job was to see that she didn't neglect herself in the pursuit. I appreciated the distraction from my heartache and the tragic irony that we both had lost a husband.

Chapter 14

On the morning of Carl's funeral, Betsy woke in a good mood. Having most of the arrangements completed seemed to lessen her burden. Today, she just wanted to concentrate completely on Carl and his extraordinary life.

An open casket service at the funeral home was to be followed by a covered dish dinner at the First Baptist Church fellowship hall. In attendance would be some of Carl's veteran friends and fellow members of the church. What went unspoken was Carl's wish to be cremated, which would take place tomorrow. So, no graveside service required.

Adjusting the strap on my patent leather pumps, I asked Betsy, "Would you like a little something to put on your stomach before we leave?"

"No." She shook her head, her silver hair catching the light. "I have a funny tummy this morning. Just some bicarbonate for me. I wouldn't want to upchuck and ruin the day in the middle of the service." She patted her belly.

It had been a rough couple of days for her with phone calls to friends and relatives, visits to the bank, and getting copies of the death certificate to the right organizations.

Fortunately for Betsy, the funeral had been prearranged and paid off for many years. This made me realize that I need to think about my own death package, someday.

Tragic as Carl's death had been for Betsy, it had been a distraction for me. Yet, I still found my mind wandering to my heartache. In the middle of being on hold with the Social Security Administration, I was fantasizing about strangling Jake. Not nice, I know. I let go before he passed out. I don't wish him dead. I just want him to hurt as much as I do right now.

I really need to check on Brian and Cindy, see how they are faring with all this change.

With Betsy's silver mane tamed into a bun, she put her black pill box hat on her head and secured it with a pearl tipped hat pin. In her smart black suit, she looked like Jackie O.

"Ready as I'll ever be," she said, trying to sound cheerful. I held the door for her and locked up, my heart heavy in my chest.

After a quiet drive, we arrived early and entered the open parlor. Carl looked at peace in the shiny black casket wearing his double breasted, stripped navy suit. There was a display of his military photos and medals among the colorful sprays of flowers. An organization that redistributes flowers to nursing homes and hospitals would pick them up at the end of the service.

Betsy straightened Carl's tie. "You look nice, darling," she whispered.

I turned and walked toward the back of the room just out of earshot to give her privacy. I busied myself, straightening the announcements and signing the register book. Hesitating on my last name I asked myself, "Am I still a Cantrell?" I suppose I am until the divorce is final.

Betsy insisted on not having a receiving line. She didn't see the point in standing alone next to Carl to shake everyone's hand. The room took on more of a party atmosphere when people arrived to stand in groups, talking and laughing about funny stories of the couple's life together.

After half an hour of ear numbing talk and laughter, the minister got everyone's attention, asking them to take a seat so that the service could begin. Betsy signaled to me to come sit by her. As I slid in next to her, she took my hand. Her hand was icy cold. She leaned toward me whispering, "Make lots of friends, Ann. Reconnect with your family or you'll be alone in the end, like me. I'm so thankful for you. These last few days would have been impossible for me if not for your help and care."

Before I could respond, the room had gone quiet. I squeezed her hand, hoping to transfer some of my body heat and reassure her.

The gentlemen from the funeral home prepared Carl's casket and closed the lid. The pallbearers, military buddies of Carl's, draped the flag over it, the bright colors signifying his service. A singer from their church followed the veterans. He sang "Beulah Land," Carl's selection.

After scripture was read and a prayer was given, the floor was opened up for people to share a memory or story of Carl's life. Several people spoke, each recalling special moments that made everyone laugh or nod their heads. It was as if Carl was briefly with us once again.

The minister closed the service with a prayer. The veterans came forward and ceremoniously folded the flag and presented it to Betsy. She hugged it to her chest and bowed her head. The same gentleman that had closed the casket announced that everyone was invited to partake of the meal provided at the church by the Bereavement Committee and that the service was now concluded.

Saying her goodbyes as she made her way out, Betsy turned to me and said lowly, "Think anyone would notice if we didn't go to the church for the meal?"

"I think you're the main attraction in this scenario." I shrugged. "Maybe you should just make an appearance."

Betsy sighed.

On the drive to the church, we were near my old neighborhood.

"Care if we make a quick stop first?" I asked.

"I welcome it." She sat up straighter.

"Well, fasten your seat belt tighter. This could be a bumpy ride," I belted out.

Betsy winced.

"Sorry, I've always wanted to say that." I smirked. She grinned for the first time in days.

As we pulled up at the front of the house, Shirley stood up and stretched her back. She had been bent over, scratching in the landscaping around the porch. Shading her eyes from the sun with her garden glove, she jumped with recognition.

"OH CRAP!" moved her lips. Dropping her tools, she ran for the front door. Her little straw hat flew off her head and landed on the walkway just as the door slammed.

"This is more fun than a solemn meal," exclaimed Betsy. "Let's go!"

After retrieving Shirley's hat, we stepped to the porch with the energy of a hound dog treeing a squirrel.

I tried the front door. It was locked. Fishing with my key ring, I inserted my old, worn house key. It didn't fit. "He has changed the locks," I said with fury. "That jerk!"

We heard voices from the other side of the door, arguing. The door popped open to reveal a red-faced Cindy.

"She's still my Mom, and this is still her house!" She was shouting at a much shorter and wider Shirley.

"Are you living here?" I asked Shirley point blank.

"Hi, sweetheart," I said to Cindy. She glared at Shirley and nodded her head yes to me.

I was livid.

"Couldn't wait until the ink was dry on the divorce papers, huh?"

Shirley shrugged her shoulders. She hadn't a leg to stand on. I plopped her straw hat onto her peroxide head. She flinched and swallowed hard.

"It's been horrible, Mom." Cindy folded her arms in a defiant stance. "Dad moved her in on Sunday right after you left. They have been carrying on for years behind our backs. It's disgusting!" She stomped her foot for effect.

Shirley found her voice. "If you could see where I came from, you wouldn't blame me a bit," she whined. "If my father wasn't beating me, my mother was. My life has been hell! Every time they have a new baby, it falls to me to take care of it. And believe me, they've had plenty. The more they have, the more they get from the government," she cried. "We lived in squalor, a stinking little trailer in the backwoods. I wish I could burn it to the ground." Her eyes expressed pain.

I was trying to picture us from above. Four women standing in a doorway in a pivotal moment in history. Betsy looked like she could run a marathon, renewed with vim and vigor. Cindy had an expression of too much information, not interested. Myself, I was feeling compassion. If any of her excuses were actually true, super hips Shirley didn't know she had exchanged one cage for another.

"Let's all go inside and sit down before the neighbors take an interest." I glanced at the street for any voyeurs, finding it empty.

"Good, I'll get us some tea," Shirley said brightly, making a dash for the kitchen.

The house was immaculately clean. There was new furniture in the living room and a new large screen television above the mantle.

Cindy, arms still folded said, "Yeah, Dad buys her whatever she wants."

Somewhere in the back of the house, a door closed. Then, we heard the sound of a car starting. Running to pull the curtains away from the front window, we see Shirley escaping down the street in a shiny, red convertible Porsche, her blonde hair flying.

"Like I said," Cindy muttered. "Whatever she wants."

"How on earth could your dad afford that car?" I asked Cindy.

"Leased," she responded.

"Let's go look through her underwear drawer," yelped Betsy. I'm not sure if she is joking, but there's no way I'm doing that in this lifetime.

Dropping my corner of the drapes. I collapsed on the overstuffed, red velvet sofa. "Are you and Brian okay, Cindy? Is there anything I can do to help make this crazy situation better?"

"Brian is never here anymore, Mom. He broke up with his girlfriend and moved in with his friend Tommy," she explained. "You remember Tommy, he lost his dad last year in Afghanistan? Tommy's mom is glad to have Brian at their house since she works so much."

I was speechless.

Betsy asked, "How does he get to school and his soccer games?"

"They fixed up Tommy's dad's old car. Tommy has his license and Brian is working on getting his. I don't know what will happen this summer. Tommy and his mom go away as soon as she is finished with classes. She teaches middle school now. They travel all summer to visit relatives that are all over the place. She hasn't invited Brian to go along, and he wants to get a job. So, I don't know if he will come back here or not. He's pretty mad at Dad and can't stand Shirley."

"I spent my summers working at Aunt Millie's farm," I volunteered.

Cindy shrugged her shoulders. "Right now, I'm not thinking past graduation."

She plopped down on the recliner. "I have finals the next two weeks and my parents have both gone crazy. There's a strange woman in my childhood home. My mother is AWOL. My father is acting like a rebellious teenager. It's all so unfair." She laid her head back and closed her eyes.

"Come stay with me," I heard myself saying.

Betsy looked over at me with concern in her eyes.

"I don't know," Cindy responded. "Can I think about it? I feel like someone sane should be here to keep watch over what's left." She gestured with open arms.

"I'm sorry for all your problems," Betsy said. "But this is still better than the 'let's all stare at the poor widow' meal would have been."

Cindy looked amusedly at her. It was good to see her face relax again.

"Oh, I should introduce you." In all the excitement, I had forgotten my manners.

"Cindy, Betsy, my friend and neighbor. We just came from her husband Carl's funeral."

"Sorry," Cindy said to Betsy. "So, that's why you're both dressed in black. It's nice to meet you. I'm so sorry for your loss."

"I'm glad to meet you too." Betsy crossed the room with open arms to give her a hug. I held my breath, thinking Cindy wouldn't like that. She stood and responded with tenderness.

"Well, who's up for pizza?" Betsy's eye sparkled. "I think my appetite is back."

Cindy obliged, punching in the numbers on her cell phone.

It could just be possible that something is blooming from all this adversity. I can physically feel the warmth growing from these two.

I think I'm having another magenta moment.

Chapter 15

Another week has gone by, and I'm still unemployed. I applied with a temp agency and have a job interview tomorrow. My skill set puts me in a good position to do most any clerical job. Trouble is, my heart just isn't in it. I really want to do something different. Just what that is, I don't know. This situation with my children has really shaken me. Cindy's graduation is just around the corner. After this summer, she starts college and things will change again for her.

I need to have a meeting with my family. If we could all just sit down and talk things out like rational people, I'm sure we could come to an agreement that would be beneficial for Brian and Cindy. Surely Jake could be reasonable when it comes to their welfare.

I was having an argument with him inside my head when my phone rang. I recognize the number. It's Aunt Millie!

"Hi, Aunt Millie."

"Hey there, my favorite niece," she said.

"Yes, and also your only niece," I responded. This is how we start all our conversations since I can remember.

"I'm so glad you called. I have been meaning to call you, but I'm always worried you'll be in the field or so busy." It sounded like a lame excuse.

"Don't give it another thought." She let me off the hook. "I'm somewhat retired at the moment. My days are filled with telling someone else what to do from a chair or on the phone."

"I can't picture you doing that. You were always so hands-on."

"I don't like laying this at your door, but I've been getting an earful from your mother. She informs me that she and my brother don't like the turn your life has taken. They insist that since I have always had more influence over you than they have, something must be done." She took a breath. "Their words, not mine. I trust you to run your own life. However, after getting a tongue lashing of right and wrong from Ruth—'I know what's best, Hopson'—I have come to the conclusion that I may need to move my plans for the future up a bit." She paused.

"I'm so sorry. My mother has always been that way. I hate that some of it fell on you. How can I explain?" I asked.

"Nothing to explain. I think I understand. Your husband wasn't treating you right and was probably messing around on the side, so you bailed. That about right?"

"Well, I didn't know about the thing on the side until after I left. But I knew something wasn't right and he was finding fault with everything I did. The children were distant and none of us were connecting," I answered. "Now, I'm an out of work, almost divorced mother who abandoned her children. Still love me?"

She laughed. I loved hearing that tinkling bell again. It was like going home.

"What's all this about future plans?" I asked, intrigued.

She replied, "You come here, see if you want to manage this place for me. Give it until the end of summer. If they'll come, bring those children of yours with you. We'll teach them to farm. Maybe it would be a good fit, maybe not, but you sure will build a bond with them. I remember how much you loved this place. Only thing I couldn't figure out is why you quit coming back. It doesn't really matter any which way. Think on it and holler back to me."

"That's a wonderful offer, Aunt Millie. I'm not sure how much of a manager I would be. Is it your health, are you okay?" I asked, worried.

"Nothing being twenty years younger wouldn't fix," she joked. "You just give it some thought. I want to see y'all just as soon as school is out." She waited.

"I will. Thank you!" My mind flashed on Betsy. "I have a favor. May I bring a friend? Her name is Betsy, and she's a recent widow. I don't think she should be left on her own just now, and I think she would be a real asset."

"Shoot, the more the merrier!" exclaimed Aunt Millie.

Could this be the answer for us? Would this be just what we all need? How could it be that simple? How on earth do I convince them to go along with such an out of the blue plan? Am I overthinking an answered prayer?

As I am hanging up, I remember all too vividly why I had quit going to Aunt Millie's . . . Jake. He and I had started dating. He had a low opinion of "country folk," as he referred to them. He didn't bother to hide his disdain. The one time I took him for a family reunion was the last. His negative comments were hurtful, and I didn't want to expose the people I loved to them. In his mind, no matter how much I tried to convince him otherwise, all country people were uneducated bumpkins.

I can imagine what his opinion of Shirley's family might be. If her story is true, not only are they redneck people, but trashy redneck people. So different from hardworking, all-American country folks. If he would give her whatever she wants, she might move them all in with him. Although, she didn't seem too keen on continuing any kind of relationship with her welfare parents. Still, I need to protect my children. This is all getting out of control.

Pushing the power button on my phone, I instructed Siri, "Call Jake Cantrell." She responded, "Calling Jake Cantrell," in her robotic voice.

"What do you want?" Jake answered belligerently. "Your settlement on the house will be automatically deposited in your account as soon as the paperwork is cleared. Might have known you'd give me hard time about it."

I ignored his rudeness. "We need to have a family meeting. I'm concerned about what effect the divorce and your moving Shirley into the house is having on Brian and Cindy."

"Interesting that you are concerned for them now that I have a new woman. What about when you abandoned them?" he retorted.

"Never mind." I hung up on him. Solutions never sprang from interactions with Jake. Maybe things have progressed to where Cindy and Brian would be open to a summer in the country.

But first, with Cindy's graduation coming up, I need to find a gift for her.

Also, I need to see if Betsy is onboard. As I'm calling, I see her walking to the mailbox. I love that my kitchen window faces the street so I'm able to see what's going on outside.

I ran to the door and opened it. "Betsy! I'm about to make you an offer you can't refuse."

Her face lit up. "What now? Don't tell me, you've won the lottery."

"No, that would be great. But it's almost that good." I ran to her. "I have a plan, and I want you to be a part of that plan!"

Her white eyebrows went up. "Let's do it!"

"You don't even know what it is." I opened my hands palms up.

"Doesn't matter. I needed something. Prayed for something." She shrugged. "I don't look a gift horse in the mouth."

"Good, because I'm going to need your help. After Cindy's graduation, we are taking her out to dinner, along with Brian. Then we, together, are going to convince them to spend the summer at my Aunt Millie's farm. I want you to come to the farm too." I paused, holding my breath, gauging her reaction.

"They just might be ready for something like that. I know I am." She gave me the thumbs up. "A summer in the county. It sounds so," she sighed, "romantic."

After sealing the deal with a hug, we went back into our condos.

I need to begin preparations. Where to start? Three months is a long time to stay somewhere other than home. Fortunately, the farm was only a couple hours away. We could come check on things within a reasonable amount of time.

First thing I need to do is get Cindy's graduation present. I have an idea. Collecting my wedding rings, I head for the jewelers to see about reconstructing them into something useful for Cindy.

As I drive down the busiest street in town, my thoughts wander to what I would miss about being in the city. Certainly, I wouldn't miss the traffic, but probably the theaters and the restaurants.

Pulling up to the jewelers, I see a red Porsche in the parking lot. You have got to be kidding me! Looking into the lighted windows of the store, I see my husband and Shirley.

My first thought is, *I could run.* I could march in there and stare at them, hoping they feel some hint of shame. Or I could key their car with the word cheater across its shiny, red exterior.

I choose door number two.

As the bell on the entry door jingled, three heads turned in my direction. The gentleman behind the counter smiled and said, "Be with you in a minute."

Jake and Shirley's eyes pop open wide as they look at me, then each other. "Excuse us," stammers Jake. "We have somewhere to be. We'll think on it and get back to you."

As he is ushering Shirley out the door, he looks at me with fury in his eyes.

Not intimidated in the slightest, I stood in front of them. Looking at Shirley face to face, I state, "You think life with your folks was a trap? Just wait. If you join your life with this one, you better prepare for neglect and boredom, and plenty of it."

Jake took her arm. Glaring at me, he pulled her outside the door. I couldn't hear what they were saying as they climbed into the little Barbie car, but there was lots of head shaking and hands flying. It looked like an argument. I felt quite pleased with myself.

"How may I help you?" asked the jeweler. He had a pleasant face.

"I would like to make some lemonade," I said, holding up my rings.

Chapter 16

Betsy and I struggled to find two empty seats in the auditorium. We were cutting it close. The weather was no help. It had stormed all afternoon, making traffic and timing difficult. Cindy's graduation ceremony was just moments from starting when a helpful usher directed us to two unoccupied seats in the front row next to the auditorium wall.

My hands were sweaty with nerves. I had canceled the temp agency interview and withdrew my name.

Over and over, I had practiced how I would approach the children with the opportunity at Aunt Millie's farm. *Please, Lord*, I silently prayed, *help me to convince them and win them back to a happy existence.*

I craned my neck, trying to find my child. There she sat in the middle of her class, staring straight ahead as if in a daze while the students around her were talking and laughing together. My poor girl.

She and Brian, who was somewhere in the building with Tommy, had agreed to have dinner afterward at the restaurant of Cindy's choice. I thought she might want to spend her graduation evening with her friends or have an invitation to a party. When she agreed to dinner, I didn't press her for any further information. If she had no plans, I didn't want to make her feel worse with a lot of questions.

As the procession of the class had their names called, I watched and waited for Cindy. I wondered if Jake and Shirley were in attendance and felt irritated at myself for letting them enter my thoughts. When they called her name, Cynthia Ann Cantrell, Betsy and I cheered and clapped our hands. I could hear Brian's distinctive whistle from somewhere in the back of the auditorium.

I sent a text to his cell phone to meet us by the front entrance afterward. He returned a text saying that he would be there. Am I getting my children back?

After the classic "looking to the future" speech was concluded, the senior class moved their tassels to indicate the completion of graduation. Mortar boards were thrown into the air to the roar of applause.

Betsy and I made our way through the celebrating crowd to Cindy. Arm in arm, she and Betsy cleared a path to our rendezvous point with Brian.

I tried to gage his mood as we approached him. Tommy was with him, looking the same with his freckles and red hair. Brian looked older and tired. He had a serious hang dog look to his face.

"Hi, Mom." He hugged me as if he hadn't seen me in forever.

"Hi, sweetheart," I garbled though a chokehold.

He released me, looking at the floor, somewhat embarrassed. "You remember Tommy?"

"Yes, hello, Tommy. Would you like to join us for dinner?"

"No, thank you, Mrs. Cantrell, I have somewhere else to be. I just wanted to make sure Brian was set for a ride." He seemed anxious to get going.

"I'm good, man," Brian said to Tommy. "Thanks, I'll see you later."

"Have a good one. Nice to see you again, Mrs. Cantrell. Congratulations, Cindy." He waved as he turned for the door.

"Brian, this is Betsy," Cindy said proudly with their arms still linked.

"Nice to meet you." Brian smiled. "Let's go eat. Where we going, Sis?"

Cindy put her lips in a mischievous grin. "I choose Chucky Cheese."

We all gasped. "Just kidding," she teased. "How does everyone feel about the Olive Garden?"

"It's your night. Wherever you say goes," I answered.

"Okay, here is what I'd really like . . . your kitchen, Mom," she said with a hopeful look.

"Surely we could scrounge something up," answered Betsy. "I still have all that food from the church ladies in my freezer."

"Alright, Mom's kitchen, it is," said Brian.

The four of us made our way to my car and talked about the speakers and the ceremony on the drive to my condo. I was so glad Betsy was there to keep the conversation going. I was in awe of having my children with me and to have them liking me again.

As we pulled into my garage, Betsy pointed out where her condo was and extended an invitation to Cindy and Brian to visit her any time. Her door was always open to them.

Cindy accompanied Betsy to her condo to collect food. Brian and I entered my kitchen.

"Mom, it's so clean and simple," he said, looking around.

"You mean, there's not much furniture or clutter?" I asked.

"Yes, it's hard to tell just who lives here. There's nothing personal."

I was trying to see my space through his eyes as Cindy and Betsy came bounding through the door carrying what looked like a casserole, French bread, and two kitchen chairs.

With the casserole defrosting in the oven, we prepared our salads from the meager selection of vegetables from my fridge. After we were all seated in the mismatched chairs, Betsy offered a blessing for our food, and we started our meal.

Brian talked about what job he thought he could get for the summer, saying they had openings to clean and serve food at the public swimming pool.

Cindy didn't mention jobs or the summer. She did ask Betsy about Carl and their life together, which Betsy was more than happy to talk about. She liked sharing his memory.

After the entree, we decided to have ice cream for our dessert.

Brian smothered his in chocolate syrup just as he had as a child.

With the dishes swishing away in the dishwasher, I asked that we all go to the living room and sit.

From my purse I pulled out my gift for Cindy. Gently removing the wrapping paper, her eyes lit up when she saw the cross with a diamond in the center on a gold chain. "It's beautiful, Mom."

"I had nineteen years of marriage, Cindy. You and Brian were the best thing to come from it, and I'm so thankful for you. This was my wedding ring set. I wanted to make something beautiful for you to cherish." My eyes were leaking again.

Brian offered to clasp the chain for her, and she let him. Sliding a small box from his pocket, he handed it to his sister. "Congratulations," he said.

Cindy opened the box and balanced the gift on her finger. "It's a keychain with my initials. Thanks, Brian. I will keep it always." She hugged her brother.

Brian lowered his head and hugged her back. "That's for your car, dorm key, or whatever."

It was Betsy's turn, and I had no idea what she was giving Cindy. I didn't really expect anything from her considering that she had just become a widow.

"I have something for both of you." She smiled.

She rose and stepped into the kitchen, retuning with a shopping bag. Out of it she pulled two gifts, handing one to Brian and one to Cindy.

"You first, Brian," Cindy said, holding her package to her chest.

Tearing open the blue tissue paper, Brian held a red leather Bible. "It was my Carl's," spoke Betsy. "If you'll notice, there are many passages underlined. There is also an entry in the front, a list of situations such as being afraid or anxious with a scripture reference to help specifically with whatever problem you might be facing."

"Thank you," Brian said softly, turning the book over in his strong, youthful hands.

"Your turn, Cindy." Betsy beamed.

Cindy tore open the pink tissue paper to reveal a collection of books. *Jane Eyre, The Scarlet Letter, Gone with the Wind, To Kill a Mockingbird,* and *Wuthering Heights.*

"Oh my, thank you." Cindy jumped and hugged Betsy.

"The classics hold up," said Betsy, winking at me.

Cindy sat down and touched each book lovingly before returning them to their wrapping. She then fingered her new necklace and looked at me with an expression I couldn't quite read.

Brian looked large in my wicker furniture, flipping through Carl's bible.

I took a deep breath. "I have some news," I started. "Aunt Millicent has made an offer." I paused for effect and to wait for their undivided attention.

"She needs someone to help manage her farm for the summer and has graciously offered to have me come do just that. I don't know a lot about managing a farm, so, I will be learning as I go. I hope to remember just what all went into doing so. I haven't worked on the farm since I was a teenager. It could be very different now, maybe modernized." I rambled on.

Betsy looked at me, clearly frustrated, sitting on the edge of her seat. "Get on with it."

I took another deep breath. "She wants the two of you to come and help work the farm, too." I braced for the onslaught of shock and disgust.

Cindy and Brian looked at each other, big eyed. They both started laughing.

"That's no weirder than what we've been experiencing," Cindy said wearily.

"Just so crazy, it might work. If you're in, I'm in!" exclaimed Betsy.

They both shrugged their shoulders. "Why not?" said Brian.

I dared not say anymore. Wouldn't want to jinx it.

After I dropped Cindy off at her car, still parked at the school, I dropped Brian off at Tommy's house.

It gave me a strange feeling to leave them in unknown territory. My drive back to the condo never seemed this lonely or the condo so empty when I arrived. I could see Betsy's lights were still on. It's late; I shouldn't disturb her.

As I got myself ready for bed, I kept thinking back over the night, replaying conversations and the faces of my children. How different they were now compared to before I moved out.

Then it occurred to me: Where was Jake tonight? Had he not attended his own daughter's graduation?

Let it go, Ann. Just let it go.

Chapter 17

The school year was over, and summertime was just around the corner. Betsy and I had made plans for closing our condos for the three months of summer, prepaying some bills, getting the water and electricity cut off, and having our mail rerouted. Brian and Cindy had packed up the things they wanted from their rooms and stored them in my garage. I didn't question them, but I suspected that they were avoiding telling their father about leaving for the summer.

All of that was answered when my cell rang while I was clearing out my desk into a portable file to take with me.

Seeing it was Jake, I let it go to voice mail.

After ranting and raving until running out the duration of a message, he called again. The second message was somewhat calmer. "I know you don't really owe me anything at this point, Ann." I hated the way he said my name, like he was spitting it out because it left a bad taste in his mouth. "But you can't really think that you can take the children off into bumpkinland and away from me, I won't let you." Then he hung up.

Well, so Jake knows. It's okay, it will work out. He just needs some time to come around. After his haze of fury clears, he will realize that there's nothing he can do. Cindy is almost eighteen, an adult. There is nothing wrong with taking your children for summer trips. People do it all the time.

Returning to my chores, a nagging thought hit me. What if he and Shirley have more children? Mentally jumping right into that scenario, I see the nightmare that Thanksgiving and Christmas holidays would be. Sometimes a good imagination is not your friend. Their kids would probably look at me and ask, "Mommy, Daddy, who is dat wady?" I shook away the tow-headed baby image.

Concentrate on here and now, Ann.

Music, I need music. I put on Canned Heat's "Going Up The Country." Don't you just love YouTube? Betsy came in my front door. Hearing the music, she started dancing. I jumped up from my desk and joined her. There we were, having our own sock hop and laughing like young girls when the song ended.

Cindy was standing in the doorway. "Really, Mom? What are you, thirteen?"

"Just inside," I answered her, still giggling. "We leave in three more days. Are you ready to go?"

"Could we move that up a day or so? Dad knows. He's so angry. Says I'm betraying him. If we can't leave sooner, can I at least stay with one of you? My suitcase is in my car." She pointed her thumb toward the door.

My poor girl. I've never seen a more pleading look on her face.

"You betcha!" Betsy hopped to her side. Turning her head away from Cindy, she winked at me. "Let's get you settled. While we're at it, we'll load up your boxes from the garage too and then we'll really be ready to make our get away."

Cindy's face relaxed in relief.

The three days passed without incident. After picking up Brian, we were a caravan, a convoy, headed for the hills. Betsy and Brian rode together in her minivan, Cindy was driving her Cabrio, and me, I'm tooling along in my new truck—well, used but new to me. Yes, I bought a little Chevy S-10, fire blue. How you like me now?

Brian and Tommy helped me get it checked out and get a good trade in for my car. The auto industry is still a man's world. It's just the way it is. If you don't want to get ripped off, you need someone with testosterone to negotiate with the salesmen.

Although, I did talk him down a couple more thousand than he wanted, and I refused the add-on costs he insisted I needed. I rode away feeling like I had made the best deal possible.

Driving toward my favorite childhood place, I felt such freedom. A fresh start, a new beginning was around every bend of the old familiar roads. My future is calling, and I am so happy to answer, *Yes. I accept.*

My only hiccup was in seeing the look of fear in my children's eyes. Where we are going is unknown to them. It would be a culture shock for them both. People here aren't attached to their phones or computers. A lot of their life will be outdoors with a great deal of physical effort expected from them, every day.

We stopped for lunch at a restaurant in the town nearest to Aunt Millie's farm. It was a little roadside diner that served burgers, soup, sandwiches, and such. Cakes were displayed in glass containers on top of the counter tops. The four of us slid into a booth with cracked burgundy seats. The ceiling tiles had rust stains from leaks. The diner had seen better days.

Cindy was pleasantly surprised to find that she had cell phone service. I didn't have the heart to tell her that she probably wouldn't when we got out on the ridge.

Betsy had a hearty vegetable soup with saltines, Brian had a burger and fries, I had the tomato soup with a grilled cheese sandwich, and Cindy had a salad, which she poked at gingerly. The food was actually pretty good and very inexpensive.

When we headed back on the road, Brian chose to ride with me. "Still liking her?" He patted the dash of my truck.

"I really do. Thanks to you and Tommy, I think I have a good one." I smiled at him.

He looked pleased as he settled back in his seat, enjoying the ride.

After eight miles of pastures, cows, barns, and country homes, we topped the hill to a view of Aunt Millie's house. "Is this it?" asked Brian, leaning toward the windshield to get a better look at the two story farmhouse with its wide porches and gabled windows. With all the outbuildings, it was quite an impressive spread.

"Actually, we've been on her property for the last mile or so. She owns several hundred acres."

I raised my eyebrows for effect.

"Dang." He laughed. "I'm going to be a cowboy."

"Yep, partner. You will be wrangling cattle." I laughed with him.

As we rolled through the last turn in the long driveway, I could see several people on the covered front porch waiting for us.

Aunt Mille came down the stairs from the porch, moving toward us. "Welcome home!" she shouted as she approached our convoy.

Opening my truck door, I was enveloped in her arms. Her warmth was so familiar.

Home, at last.

"Don't worry about unloading; my guys will get your things sorted," she insisted. "Come meet some of the folks you'll be working with and some of our neighbors." She looked so aged. Her face was crinkled. "You're home, and tonight we celebrate." She beamed, tears forming in her worn eyes as she cupped my face with tenderness.

All the work hands greeted us as we passed them on their way to empty our things from our vehicles. You could tell that the group of weathered men knew each other well by the way they were kidding and pushing each other as they set about gathering our things.

Carrying my two pieces of luggage and electronics bag like they weighed nothing was the tallest and oldest of the men. Aunt Millie introduced him as Ranger Adams, the foreman.

Shifting my things to one arm, he lifted his cap and acknowledged me with a little bow of his head, revealing jet black hair. "Ma'am." His voice had the timbre of a baritone.

He gave orders to the other men as to where things were to be placed. Among the four of them, they had all our things nicely stored inside in short order. My things went to my old room, dubbed the lilac room; Cindy's to the sunflower room; Brian's to the bird room; and Betsy's to the fleur de Luis room, all on the second floor.

Aunt Millie motioned toward the people on the porch. "The Clark family live just over the next ridge. They run sheep on their spread." He was portly, and she was a tiny thing with shoe button eyes.

"The Andersons live on the farm adjacent to us. They have a campground and lake access that keeps them hopping." They looked like Roy Rodgers and Dale Evans, a perfectly matched couple.

Then she turned to someone sitting in the swing. Smiling she said, "I think you remember Bond Winston." She looked at me, big eyed.

Standing up from the swing was a memory from my tender teenage years. All the girls had been crazy for him. He was still handsome, blond hair gleaming in the afternoon sun, his smile just as bright and his dark eyes shining. "Good to see you again, Annie. You grew into quite a woman," he teased.

My knees went wobbly. Mentally, I kicked myself. *Say something.* "It's nice to meet all of you." I hoped I didn't sound as lame to them as I did to myself.

"Our children are all down at the pond if you'd like to join them," spoke the small but strong Mrs. Clark. "We have two sons, and the Andersons have a son and a daughter," she explained.

Cindy and Brian looked curiously at their surroundings. "It's just next to the barn," pointed Aunt Millie. They glanced at each other and started off toward the barn just a little farther down the gravel driveway. Cindy looked back at me, as if checking that I was okay.

Betsy had been hanging back, watching everyone.

"I'm so sorry, everyone, this is Betsy." I pulled her next to me. "We have adopted each other. She is going to spend the summer here too," I said breathless.

"Well, Betsy," Aunt Millie cackled, "looks like I'm going to have a new friend. It's good to have someone more my age around. We can share our old war stories." She put an arm around Betsy.

"I feel at home already." Betsy grinned.

Chapter 18

After a night of storytelling, laughter, and home-cooked food, we all fell into our soft beds for some much-needed sleep. It was so quiet, I could almost hear the quietness. I kept willing my eyes to close, but they kept popping back open.

I could hardly believe Aunt Millie had kept my room the same as when I stayed there as a child. The subtle lilac wallpaper was a bit faded, but the white lace curtains were just as bright and billowing as I remembered—the deep cherry dresser, bedside table, desk and headboard all gleaming from years of polish. So much of life has happened since I slept under the tin roofed house.

My brain kept running over the conversation and the characters we had met today. Brian and Cindy behaved in the same manner as myself. While everyone else was so animated, as if they were trying to one up each other, we three were observers with the occasional head nod or smile.

Betsy was in rare form. She had everyone in tears of laughter, telling them stories of herself and Carl and some of the pranks they would pull. It made me wish I had met them sooner; my life might have been very different.

Bond Winston, who (surprise!) was an attorney, bowed out early, saying that he had a case first thing in the morning, but not before he made me a bit uncomfortable with staring at me a little too long.

The foreman, Ranger Adams, seemed to miss nothing. He saw Bond out to his car and looked at me protectively when he returned. His crew sat up taller when he reentered the room. I couldn't tell if it was fear or respect, but it was noticeable. I know who he reminds me of—John Wayne. Not so much in looks, but in his mannerisms.

After everyone noticed Brian yawning, the Anderson and Clark families left with a promise to show us around their place the next day.

Of the three neighbor boys, the Clarks' son was more Brian's age. Gil, short for Gilman, his mother's maiden name, was talking Brian up about the 4-H club and showing his sheep at the county fair. Brian politely listened but didn't show much interest. He asked Gil a lot of questions about the livestock, specifically the cattle and horses. I could see his ears perk up when Gil told him that they use ATVs to get around instead of horses.

Everywhere Cindy went or sat, the Anderson's daughter, Megan, was her shadow. Cindy tolerated her constant questions about Cindy's school, car, hair, friends, clothes, etc. She was excited to show Cindy the pool they have at the campground and the boat dock at the lake.

Megan's mother reined her in several times, saying that she had the curiosity of a cat.

After a few more moments of sleepless struggle, I got out of bed and sat in a ladder-back chair at the window. Looking outside, I remember how dark real dark can be. No city lights out here, folks. As the clouds parted, the half-moon revealed itself, making long shadows from the trees and the outbuildings. I could see the main road just over the rise. It looked like a gray ribbon.

Cracking my window open just slightly, I hear nature's song. Birds and insects were singing a lullaby, giving me a peace I haven't known in some time.

Crawling back into bed, I pull the soft quilt up to my chin and drifted off, sighing, with a smile on my face.

I awoke to the sound of voices and dishes rattling and the wonderful aroma of bacon.

After making my bed, I grabbed my jeans and a T-shirt and head for the bathroom down the hallway. Knocking on the door, I gratefully find it unoccupied. I hurriedly completed washing and dressing. After returning my robe and pajamas to my room, I hopped down the stairs toward the aroma.

Betsy was standing at the stove of the spacious kitchen, turning bacon in an iron skillet. Cindy and Brian were sitting with Aunt Millie at the large oak, oval table in the middle of the room, having coffee. "Good morning," sang out Betsy and Aunt Millie in harmony.

We all chuckled. "I trust you slept well?" asked Aunt Millie.

"Yes, eventually, I did. What's on the agenda for today?" I asked as I opened the familiar cherry knot wood cabinet to get a coffee mug.

Aunt Millie went down a mental list of chores. Betsy joined us at the table with a stack of pancakes and plate of bacon. While we ate, Aunt Millie gave out our assignments. It was good to see my children with an appetite again, especially Cindy.

Brian was to go out with Gil for an ATV training ride to check the cattle in the south pasture. Cindy wanted, of all things, to learn to drive the tractor. Betsy was to become more familiar with the kitchen and help Aunt Millie prepare lunch for the family and the work hands. My job was to look at the books to learn more about managing the farm. I was a little disappointed to be doing office work until Aunt Millie ended my assignment with "and mucking out the barn this afternoon." She gave me a wink.

Betsy shooed us all away when we offered to help with the dishes. "Get out of here, you all have plenty to do. This is my job!" Her eyes were twinkling.

Brian headed out to find Gil waiting on the porch for him, and Cindy went to the barn to look over the tractor and wait for her lesson.

Opening the door to the office, I flipped on the light. After a couple of hours of reading notes, checking computer data entries, and looking through files, I knew I had to reorganize the entire system. I hoped to do it without ruffling Aunt Millie's feathers. The state of the office now would make it terribly difficult to get anything done efficiently. She still had records in the bulging files from 30 years back. I needed storage boxes or permission to purge. Fortunately, there was a strong Wi-Fi signal. They must have built towers. I remind myself, it is the twenty-first century.

I've found that Aunt Millie's farm supplies businesses with many diverse products. Herbs and starts for planting fill the greenhouses. The fields were full of corn, soybeans, and wheat. Some fields were left to grow grass for hay. My favorite field would be the sunflowers. By the end of summer, they start to droop, heavy with seed. During the summer, our vegetables would supply several booths at the local farmer's market. Aunt Millie's personal garden is just a five-minute walk from the front porch. It would supplement our meals and provide vegetables to be canned for the winter months.

I'm hoping that orders and payment will eventually become electronic, simplifying communications. The change may be a slow progression. I would need to contact each account. Some will be glad to do business electronically, while others will want to remain old school with the personal touch and paper statements.

As I worked, I could hear laughter from the kitchen. Aunt Millie and Betsy were really getting along.

Betsy rang the dinner bell at noon. I could hear the voices and footsteps of the workers coming into the house. I hadn't accomplished as much as I would have liked, only making it into the "H" file drawer. Various cardboard boxes were holding the pulled files I deemed too old to keep. Drawers "A" through "G" were breathing a sigh of relief, now holding paperwork from only seven years back.

Rubbing my eyes, weary of reading for four hours, I headed to the kitchen for lunch. Betsy had created a feast. We were eating buffet style—soup beans, greens, fried chicken, and cornbread. The work hands filled their plates and headed outside to sit at the table on the porch.

Cindy and Brian followed their lead. They teased Cindy about running into a fence post with the tractor. "That thing needs power steering," she said, defending herself.

"She'll get the hang of it; she's already a better driver that any of you were your first time out," Ranger said with a grin. The three young men hesitantly agreed.

"You should have seen Brian on the ATV. He's like a daredevil on that thing," said Gil.

"I was just having a little fun," said Brain.

It was so good to hear them all talking like friends.

Chapter 19

My body has gone soft. After mucking out the stalls in the barn, I discovered muscles aching that I didn't remember having. The saying "what doesn't kill you makes you stronger" would definitely apply. There were only three stalls to clean out. It has to be done every day. By the end of summer, I will be a fierce muscle woman. I don't want to think about how I will feel in the morning.

After I finished the chore, I covered the stall floors with wood shavings and replenished the water and feed for the horses. Dumping the last wheelbarrow load on the dung heap, I hosed it off along with the tools and my rubber boots.

After putting everything away, I circled the corral and climbed the rail fence to sit and watch the horses grazing in the field. The two mares, both rescues, looked like sisters, chestnut red with differently marked faces. Commodore was a palomino, so beautiful and regal with his flowing mane. He was Aunt Millie's. Curiosity brought him over to me. I spoke to him gently as I softly scratched his neck. He tolerated me for a bit and then lost interest, returning to prancing around the field and munching grass.

I heard the roar of the tractor as Cindy and Ranger were pulling into the other end of the barn. Hopping off the fence I walked out into the open to see her driving with his standing on the back end pointing and instructing as she expertly pulled in and cut the motor. She turned, giving Ranger a high-five. I don't think I have ever seen her do that. She caught sight of me.

"Mom! Did you see that? I'm getting pretty good at it. We are going to hook up the cut up the ground thing tomorrow." Her face was glowing.

"Disk Harrow," offered Ranger as he pointed to it sitting to the right against the wall.

"Thank you, Ranger, I'll see you in the morning. Bye, Mom." She was off, running toward the house. She turned back toward us, running backward. "I'm heading over to see Meagan and help clean the pool at the campground. See you at supper." Hopping into her Cabrio, she cranked it up and headed down the road, blowing up a cloud of dust.

"She seems to be taking to the country life," I said to Ranger.

"Sometimes, all you need is a change, a new start," he said, looking at me wisely.

Before he could notice my flushing cheeks, I quickly changed the subject. "Would you check the stalls? It's been a while, and I may have forgotten a step or two." I walked around to the other side of the barn as he followed.

Poking his head in, he glanced around. "Looks fine, just fine. One of the hands would be glad to take this chore on if you'd like." He cocked an eyebrow at me.

"Maybe if I have a day that I can't get to it. That was my job when I spent holidays and summers here, since I can remember, except for a long period of time that I couldn't come back. I kind of enjoy it, if that makes any sense." I shrugged.

I turned back to face him, finding him staring at me. He nodded his head then looked at the ground. "I'd better get back to it."

Walking toward his truck, he took a red bandana out of his back pocket. After swiping his face, he tied it around his neck. "Ann," he said softly, sitting in his truck.

I looked up at him.

He studied my face for a moment. "I'm awfully glad you and the children are here. You've already made such a difference." His voice was kind and compassionate.

My mouth went dry. It was one of those moments you store in your memory bank to keep so you can take it out later and remember the feeling.

Looking into those deep blue eyes, all I could do was nod yes as my heart pounded. I'm finally getting something right. I feel respected and validated with his approval. Things were going to be okay.

Giving a tip of his cap bill, he pulled away.

I watched as he headed toward the north field where the crew were clearing away debris from downed trees and mending fences today. I waited as the truck got smaller and smaller, finally disappearing over the horizon.

A cool breeze blew back my hair, reminding me it was still spring. I inhaled the fresh air and felt invigorated. Turning to the west, I could see storm clouds gathering. Trekking back to the barn, I opened the corral gate so the horses could get back into the barn should the storm came our direction. Commodore didn't wait for an invitation as he sauntered on by me with the admiring mares in his wake. They huddled together inside the barn while I closed the corral gate and opened their stall doors. Each entered as if they had been waiting for the comfort and food inside. Stomping and neighing, as if to say thank you, they began eating.

After securing the outside doors, I left the barn for the office. Entering the mudroom, I pulled off my rubber boots and slid into my tennis shoes. Using Aunt Millie's grime removing lye soap, I scrubbed until I felt sufficiently clean. I could smell something delicious floating in the air.

Stepping into the kitchen, I saw Betsy pulling a pie out of the oven. "What have we here?"

"Strawberries, fresh picked this morning." Her mouth made the shape of an O. "Can you imagine? I just walked right out below the old spring house and picked them and made a pie. Isn't that a hoot?" She laughed.

"I think we should go exploring, no telling what other treasures we may find," I responded as I got a glass from the cabinet and filled it with water from the refrigerator. "I didn't realize how thirsty I was."

Fanning the pie with her oven mitt, Betsy said, "I'm loving it here. I think Brian and Cindy are, too. How do you think things are going?"

"It may be too soon to tell. I think we will know in a week or two. It's a really big change, and working so much might get old by then," I said as I sat at the table to rest my back.

Thunder clapped, making us both jump. The sound of the rain was almost deafening against the tin roof.

"Where's Aunt Millie?" I asked loudly to be heard over the pounding.

"She's lying down a while, said she wasn't feeling so hot."

My heart skipped a beat. I had never known her to even take a nap during the day. I put my water glass in the sink and hurried to her room across the hall from the office.

Lightly tapping on her door, I got no response. I turned the knob slowly, trying to not make a lot of noise. As the door creaked open, I saw her lying very still on the bed. Relief spread over me when I saw her chest rising and falling. I eased back out the door and let her rest.

While standing in the hallway, I sent a text to Cindy and Brian, wondering where they were taking shelter from the storm. I got an emoji from Brian with the thumbs up, an "okay" sign. Cindy sent a text that she and Meagan were making cookies and she would bring me some.

Feeling relieved, I headed back to the office to tackle a few more files before suppertime.

Aunt Millie seemed fine at supper. While passing the mashed potatoes, she joked about becoming a lazy-bones. It was a relief to see her looking refreshed and hearty.

Chapter 20

Our days are starting to resemble somewhat of a routine. Each morning after breakfast, I spend an hour or so in the office answering the phone, working on accounts and emails for orders. On Fridays, I do payroll and the bills.

Ranger and I have a meeting each evening as to what needed attention the next day and scheduling the hands. I always look forward to it. Nothing seemed to escape his watchful eye. Even a leaning fence post didn't have a chance. It was repaired ASAP.

One day a week, usually Saturday, I go into town, hitting the co-op for supplies and the grocery for food and other items. We kept a running list on the fridge for everyone to jot down what they need. It is always more fun for me if one or more of the family go along. That gives us a chance to talk and for me to gage how they are doing.

On Sundays, we attend the little country church. Great improvements have been made since my youth. Indoor restrooms were a pleasant surprise along with a block building that had become a fellowship hall, complete with a kitchen.

The ancient graveyard was like a family history lesson for the children. Brian and Cindy were full of questions as to how they were related to them, some of them I could answer. The rest, I told them to ask their Aunt Millie.

Sundays and Mondays are days off for the hands. So it's up to Cindy,

Brian, and myself to see to the livestock. With Sunday being a day of rest, neighbors come in the afternoon to sit on the porch and visit. They all leave when the sun begins to sink in the west.

Mondays are laundry day. Everyone strips their beds and leaves their laundry in the mudroom that also houses the washer and dryer.

I remember back when Aunt Millie had a wringer washer in there and we put the clothes outside on the line to dry. Sometimes we would get scolded for running in between the sheets while playing tag. All she ever said was, "Here now." We knew what she meant and would move our game somewhere else, usually the barn.

July had arrived, and we were halfway into the season. All would change soon when the summer would wind down. We were constantly harvesting one field or another. The end of our time at the farm was looming. It would soon be the time to make decisions. Brian would need to go back to school, and Cindy needed to confirm her choice about college. Betsy and I would need to make decisions too. Our condos couldn't sit empty forever.

Betsy is a powerhouse when it comes to her canning skills. Rows of vegetables are lined up in the cellar like glass jar soldiers. She has also taken over the chores of laundress and housekeeper. In the evenings and at mealtime, she's an entertainer. Her enthusiasm and lightheartedness are contagious.

Each day, with the exception of Sunday, the mail usually came around noon. Our mail carrier would come bee-bopping down the drive, slide up the mailbox, and deposit the daily offering. With a friendly wave and U-turn, she laid down a cloud of dust back to the main road.

Today's mail included a large manila envelope, addressed to me, with stamped forwarding information. Suspecting what it might be, I hoped to have private moment to look it over. I tried to hide it under my arm and slip back into the office. Unfortunately, it was during everyone's lunch break and all eyes were eager to know what had come in the mail.

I handed off everything addressed to the hands to Ranger, without a remark. He looked at me with curiosity in his eyes. Usually, that's not how we handle their mail. The hands have a box just for them at the bunk house. Anxious to see what was inside, I gripped the mystery envelope tighter and stepped into the house. Aunt Millie followed me to the office.

"Hi, is there something you need for me to do?" I asked with a rasp, feeling anxious.

"Open it," she said as she pulled up a wooded stool next to the door.

Skipping my usual step of using a letter opener. I ripped it open across the tape and stamps. "It's just what I thought it was, my divorce papers. I guess I'm single."

Looking up I notice Betsy, Cindy, and Brian standing in the doorway. I couldn't help myself. They all blurred as tears formed in my eyes and flooded over.

"It's okay, Mom," Cindy whispered into the room.

Brian came to me and got down on his knees and held me while I sobbed. "No one blames you, Mom. What happened wasn't good."

"That's right!" Betsy said emotionally, wiping her face with her apron.

Brian released me and I stood up, dabbling my nose and eyes with a tissue. "You all are the greatest. I'm so blessed. The people I love the most are all right here, supporting and loving me. I don't know why I'm crying. It's like someone died. That's the only way I can explain what I'm feeling. It's like a death. I'm fine, really. I knew this was coming. I just didn't know I would feel anything when it finally happened. I should be relieved, but I only feel . . . a loss."

Turning toward them, Aunt Millie requested that she could speak alone with me. After each one gave me a hug, the three of them left the office. Aunt Millie closed the door softly behind them.

"I have some things we need to talk about," she said sitting again on the stool. "Not to take away from your grief, but there's something you need to know before you make your decisions from this moment forward. Since you are single and no longer tied to Jake, I can start putting things in your name, if you agree to my plans. My children have their inheritance spelled out in my will and are not interested in this farm for themselves or my grandchildren." She cleared her throat. "Swap seats with me, dear, this stool is killing my back."

As we exchanged seats, she opened a file drawer and pulled out a strong box. Taking a key from the desk drawer, she opened it. After ruffling through papers, she pulled out the one she had been searching for.

"This here is the deed to this farm. It was nearly lost during the depression before it was handed down to John and again when times were lean during a couple of years of drought. My hardest struggle was when my John died. But, somehow, through the grace of God, I was able to muddle through. I think seeing that hardship was what made my children not want to be farmers. Aaron has asked that I would consider selling and move to live with his family in Virginia. You know he's a career Navy man now." She shook her head. "No son with a growing family should take care of his parent, too. Besides, I would really miss being home." She smiled. "I just wanted to show you where this was, just in case something should happen. My will is in there, too."

"What could happen? Is there something you aren't telling me?" I said, concerned.

Aunt Millie hesitated. She replaced the strong box and the key to the desk. Then setting her mouth in a thin line, she said, "I have been diagnosed with heart disease." She studied my face, braced for my reaction. "If I don't take precautions, it could wipe me out in a moment's notice. I'm too old and it's too late to do anything about it. So, no surgery or preventions will help."

I stood up. Then sat back down. "No! What are the doctors saying? You are in someone's care?"

"Yes." She shook her head. "They have all this medication for me to take and want me to slow down. I see them every so often."

Then it came to me. "That's where you and Mrs. Anderson have been going?"

Several times over the last couple of months, Cindy had gone to help Meagan when Aunt Millie and her mother had gone into town.

"I'm so sorry." It was her turn to cry. I had never seen my aunt, a pillar of strength, cry. It broke my heart.

After she had gathered herself, she continued. "If you are agreeable, I want to put the farm in your name. I'm hoping you will stay on to run things at least until I'm gone. I have already asked my children if it is agreeable to them, and from what I can gather, they are relieved that it will remain in the family without being a responsibility to them."

I could tell that it pained her to not have her children interested in being a part of something she had worked her whole life to keep running.

"I'm not sure what Brian and Cindy are wanting, but we will talk about it tonight. It seems we all have some decisions to make. I want to help you any way that I can. I don't know enough about your heart situation. But I know stress doesn't help anything. So, I want you to be assured that I really love what I'm doing now. I feel like I'm making a difference, not just for myself, but for my children, Betsy, and so many others. I hope that gives you consolation, knowing that your future and the farm will be secure."

Aunt Millie's expression was one of relief. "I think I may go lie down for a while," she said as she stood. When she got to the door, she turned and looked at me, searching my face. "You were always like one of my own, and this was always your home. No matter where you went, it was, and is, where you belong. It's good to belong somewhere."

"Thank you," was all I could think to say.

Walking her to her room, I softly closed the door behind her. I could hear her weeping. It made me consider the cost of investing my life into something that carried so much responsibility. Could I really do this? The more I do, the less she will have on her and the longer I will have her guidance and council. Setting my jaw, I am determined to make this the best farm in the whole county.

Pressing my ear to her door, I couldn't hear her crying anymore, as I say a silent prayer of peace and good health for her.

Chapter 21

After Aunt Millie's health revelation, I entered the office and switched the phone over to the answering machine. Scanning over my divorce papers, I find that I indeed would have no more responsibilities to Jake and joint custody of Brian and Cindy. I should feel lighter, but I only feel sadness. If only Aunt Millie were okay. Why, God? It's so unfair. I needed some air and time to think.

Making my way into the kitchen, I find Betsy and Cindy at the sink washing dishes.

"Mom, you okay?" asked Cindy.

I thought of Aunt Millie's news and wondered when she would share that. My divorce is enough for today. I would leave that to Aunt Millie for when she was ready to tell everyone.

"I will be," I answered. "Could you two hold down the fort a while? I think I'll go for a little walk."

"Sure," answered Cindy.

"Take as long as you need," answered Betsy.

Making my way past the barn, Commodore came up to me, nuzzling my pocket. "No apples today, my friend." I was sorry to disappoint him. The mares had gone to their forever home, giving rides to handicapped children at a ranch just outside of Nashville. Commodore was probably getting awful lonesome without their admiration. "How about a ride?" I suggested to him. His ears perked up. I hadn't ridden him yet. So, I knew I'd be taking a chance that he might throw me or not cooperate. If he was gentle enough for Aunt Millie, it should be okay.

Putting on his blanket, harness, and saddle was a bit of a problem. I could tell he was either excited or anxious. He had a little trouble being still.

Slipping my tennis shoe into the stirrup, I swung my other leg over. I had forgotten how high off the ground you are when sitting on a horse. I gave him a little nudge with my heels and made a clicking noise indicating I was ready to go. It was all coming back to me.

With a slow and easy gait, we made our way into the open field. I had a destination in mind, my old thinking spot. Just over the next ridge was a valley with trees and a brook if we had recent rains. There, my favorite tree lived, a mighty evergreen called the Georgia pine. It was surrounded with soft needles and green moss. I had many childhood naps and imaginative cloud watching there. Memories came to me of my cousins Aaron and Emily calling out, "I see a dog. That one looks like a dinosaur." Sometimes we agreed, sometimes we argued. Funny how the same cloud would look like something different to each of us.

Commodore seemed to sense where we were going. Either that or he smelled the water and looked forward to a refreshing drink.

Topping the horizon, I halted Commodore so I could take in the view. The rolling hills, blue sky, and lazy, floating clouds were breathtaking. A hawk was making wide circles overhead. Commodore stomped his impatience.

"Okay, boy." We continued down the slope.

Rounding several boulders at the bottom of the ravine, I caught a glimpse of my spot. It was still intact. I was so relieved to find that time, weather, nor man had taken away the majesty.

Dismounting and tethering Commodore to a small shady cedar next to the water, I sat beneath the tree on the moss and quieted my mind. Commodore occasionally checked that I was still there while drinking and munching nearby tuffs of grass.

Can I do this? Aunt Millie did. She single-handedly ran a farm and finished raising her family after Uncle John passed. Somehow, I knew the answer. Of course I could do this. Maybe, if I'm very lucky, Cindy or Brian will want to take it over someday. I could hope that, but not too much. I want them to have the future they want, not one that is pushed on them. Checking for ants or other inhabitants, I lay back into the moss. *Farm life*, I exhale, feeling relaxed for the first time in, well, forever. That cloud looks like a carrot. My stomach growled, reminding me, with everything that had happened, I had skipped lunch. I laughed out loud, startling Commodore. After an hour or so, we made our way back to the barn. I got an apple from the house and let Commodore munch on it while I gave him a good brushing. He was very affectionate, rubbing his head against my shoulder. I think he's finally getting accustomed to my presence.

At supper, things were subdued and somewhat strained. Brian, looking tanned and fit, concentrated on his food, finishing quickly, and asked to be excused. Gil and some of his friends were still out bailing hay, and he wanted to go help them before it got dark. Cindy poked at her food and kept shifting in her chair as if she couldn't get comfortable. Betsy kept looking from me to Cindy between bites and glimpsing curiously at Aunt Millie. "Something's up," she said, breaking the silence. "What gives?" she asked, laying down her fork.

Aunt Millie reluctantly told them of her condition. With stares of unbelief, Cindy and Betsy took it all in. In unison, they both rose from their seats and came to Aunt Millie's side. "So sorry," they were repeating. Aunt Millie was having none of it.

"You two, please sit down and finish your supper. I'm going to be just fine. We will get through this. So, if you feel led, please share the information. Lord knows, it's easier than my having to repeat the telling of it. The more I say it out loud, the scarier it gets. I just as soon not ever say it to another living soul." She hit the table with both hands flat, putting an end to the discussion.

"This has been the stinkiest day ever!" Cindy yelled angrily.

"True that!" seconded Betsy, slamming her hands on the table.

Together, the three of them started slamming down their hands.

In mid laugh, I began choking on a mouthful of cornbread. Coughing and gagging, I drank my iced tea to clear my airway. "You all are a mess!" I hollered and joined in the beat, hitting my hands as hard as I could.

Ranger poked his head inside the door, "Everything alright in here?"

"We are pounding it out, Ranger! It's all good." He grinned, content with that response, and left us to our insanity.

Chapter 22

The next morning, I dragged myself to the table for breakfast. I had a restless night, imagining all the responsibility of running the farm. I'd like to have a conversation with Aunt Millie and get her take on just how she managed it all while raising two children on her own.

Cindy grabbed a biscuit and mumbled something about lifeguarding at the Andersons' campground as she headed for the door.

"Be sure to wear sunscreen!" I called over my shoulder. Brian had come in last night from working the hay, looking red as a beet. It had been such a scorcher of a day. They had shed their sweat-soaked shirts, trying to stay cool. Fortunately, Aunt Millie had a homemade ointment for me to smear over his tender skin.

"Does anyone know the forecast?" I asked the wilted group around the table.

Betsy shrugged, Aunt Millie shook her head, and Brian looked up at the ceiling.

"I think they are calling for rain this weekend," he responded, looking doubtful.

"If we don't get rain soon, we may have to irrigate," I suggested.

All three heads nodded in agreement.

"I'll have Ranger get the water tanks ready, just in case," I said, thinking out loud.

We all scattered to our chores. Betsy began clearing the table, Aunt Millie headed to the porch to water her hanging plants, and Brian slipped on his boots in the mudroom and grabbed a cap off the hook before heading out to his ATV. Me, I headed to the office to answer some emails and send some invoices. That being done, I headed outside to check on the HVAC.

It's so hot; if only there was a breeze. The first floor of the house was cooler than the second floor. The air unit was struggling to keeping up with the demand. I say a little prayer for relief as I watch the fan turning in the unit.

At lunch time, Aunt Millie prepared herself a glass of buttermilk with cornbread and went to sit on the shady side of the porch.

I had very little appetite but grabbed an apple off the sideboard and joined her.

As she spooned her concoction, I watched, fascinated. I never could bring myself to drink buttermilk. "Is that on your heart healthy diet?" I teased her.

"I'm old, I'm dying, I'll eat what I want," she said defiantly.

"Aunt Millie, how did you do it, how did you run this farm and raise Aaron and Emily all by yourself?" I asked.

She laughed her tinkling bell sound. "I don't know." Sitting down her glass, she turned to me. "Think back on something really hard. Something you can't believe you accomplished. Like getting your degree while raising Cynthia and Brian. That couldn't have been easy. You just kept at it and did the best you could, every day. Sure, some things may have been neglected. Probably your housework or yard work, but you did it. And my guess is that you didn't have a lot of spousal help." She picked up her glass and continued eating.

I sat back, taking in the view of the sunlit, rolling hills. I could see our sunflower field with the bowed flower heads, heavy with seeds. The cows in the adjacent field gathered under a large oak shade tree next to the ever-shrinking pond.

"It's so beautiful here." I sighed.

"Yep," agreed Aunt Millie. "It sure is."

The roar of an ATV broke the moment of peace. Gil came bounding toward the porch.

"Brian is hurt," he shouted. "Come quick!"

Betsy came running outside, wiping her hands on her apron.

"How bad is it?" I asked, my mind spinning.

"Mr. Anderson is with him. He was an EMT. Says he may have a concussion, and his left arm is broken pretty bad. They are loading him up to take him to the hospital." He took a breath.

"How did it happen?" I asked.

"He come over a rise too quick, and the ATV rolled over on him." He shrugged. "I tried to warn him. I'm awful sorry, Ms. Cantrell."

"Betsy?" I turned to find her right behind me. "Would you please call Cindy and tell her what's happened and to keep an eye on things here until I get back?"

Aunt Millie looked a little pale. "Oh, Ann, if anything happens to that boy, I'm so sorry, honey."

"I got this, you need to get to the hospital," Betsy insisted.

Bounding back inside, she was but a second before returning with my purse. "You don't worry about anything here." She handed me my purse and keys.

"May I go with you?" asked Gil. "I'll get a ride back with Ranger or Mr. Anderson."

I nodded my agreement to Gil. Running backward toward my truck, I called to Betsy and Aunt Mille. "I'll call you from the hospital."

"Go!" They both shooed me away with their waving hands.

I barely remember the ride to the hospital. Driving as fast as humanly possible, I was straightening out the curves on the narrow road. It was a miracle that no one was coming the other direction.

Parking the truck with a screech, we ran into what was more a glorified clinic than a hospital. I was praying that they would have what was needed to help Brian.

The Emergency Room was on the main floor. I imagine the second and third floors are patient rooms. Ranger and Mr. Anderson were in the waiting area. They both stood as I approached them.

"He's fine, Ann." Ranger spoke first, assuring me.

"He has a pretty bad fracture just below the elbow on his left arm," indicated Mr. Anderson. "The bone didn't come through. We isolated it as quickly as possible. He was unconscious for just under a couple of minutes. So, he should have a complete recovery. We weren't sure about insurance. They need to talk to you at the desk." He pointed to the two staff members at the reception desk.

"Thank you, Mr. Anderson." I patted his arm. "I'm so grateful you were there."

He shyly looked at the floor. "Glad to be of help. Me and the Misses are awful fond of the boy. He's a good kid, just needs to slow down a little on those hills." He grinned.

Nodding to him and Ranger I made my way to the reception desk where Gil was waiting for me. "When can I see my son, Brian Cantrell?" I asked anxiously.

"They just finished setting his arm," responded the perky receptionist. "He will be getting a scan after that to check for any other problems, since there is a possibility of a concussion. May I have your insurance information, please?"

Digging through my purse, I found my wallet and produced the only insurance card I have, which is through Jake's business, hoping he hadn't canceled it or dropped our coverage.

"The primary carrier is Jake Cantrell." The receptionist smiled up at me. "We will need to contact him for confirmation."

"Sure, whatever you need." Dread sunk to the bottom of my stomach like a stone dropping in a lake. I reluctantly gave her Jake's number and watched in wide-eyed horror as she punched it out and spoke to him.

After answering a barrage of questions, she completed the call with a polite, yet stiff, "Thank you." Looking at me with a mix of curiosity and sympathy she said, "I have everything I needed. I'll file the insurance claim for you."

Letting out the breath I had been holding, I asked, "May I go back and see my son now?"

"Yes." She pointed to the right. "Through those doors, and to the left."

"Thank you." I called over my shoulder as Gil and I went through the doors.

Brian was in the second cubicle, sporting a bright green cast that ran from his elbow to his wrist. "Hi, Mom," he said, a little too happily. Pain killers.

"Hi, sweetheart." I leaned over and hugged his head. "So glad to see you in one piece."

"I'm fine. They want to keep me overnight, but I'm good to go, got to get back on the horse that threw me," he joked.

"Slow your roll there, Top Gun. It's not the time now, but I think we need to have yet another conversation about safety before you take off." I smoothed down his sun-streaked hair.

My poor boy. With the sunburn and bruises, he looked completely tragic.

I felt my cell phone buzz in my purse. Looking at the screen, I recognize Jake's number.

As Gil stepped up to the bed and started reminiscing about how much air Brian had cleared, skyrocketing over the hill, I excused myself and stepped into the hallway.

"Hello." I closed my eyes and leaned against the wall, bracing myself.

"Is Brian okay?" Jake asked with genuine concern.

"Yes, thankfully, it wasn't bad. He has a broken arm and some bruising. They want to keep him overnight in case he might have a concussion."

"Thank God!" he responded. "Do I need to come?" he asked softly.

"Only if you want to. Would you like to talk to him?" I asked.

"Sure," he answered. I could hear squeaking in the background. The sound of him standing up from his office chair.

Stepping back into the room, I interrupted Gil's interpretation of how Brian looked laying on the ground. I asked Brian, "Would you like to talk to your dad?"

He extended his good hand to take the call. I settled myself into one of the gray plastic chairs next to the privacy curtain and listened as Brian retold the story of his launch into space and crash to the ground. Brain then listened and replied with a yes here, a no there, and concluded his phone conversation by handing the phone back to me.

Not knowing if he had disconnected, I put the phone to my ear. "Ann," came back Jake's voice.

"Yes," I replied.

"I don't like what's going on here. He needs to come home. You're going to get him killed. How could you be so negligent?" he said angrily.

"It was an accident. I'm not going to argue with you. Brian will heal and when school starts in the fall, he will decide where he wants go live," I insisted.

"Whoa, wait a minute here, what are you saying? That he might not come back, even when summer is over? That wasn't the plan."

At that moment, the doctor came into the cubicle.

"Got to go, Jake, the doctor is here. We'll get to this later," I said quickly.

"You bet we will!" he shouted.

After we got Brian his scans, he was placed in a room. Even though the scans were clear, they wanted to keep him overnight for observation.

Ranger, Mr. Anderson, and Gil came shuffling in to say their goodbyes and head out. I called the farm and let everyone know that he was doing well.

Brain found a baseball game to watch, and I busied myself with making notes on what to do next as we settled in for the duration.

I needed a new plan for the end of summer. We needed to have a family meeting.

Decisions, decisions.

Chapter 23

After a sleepless night of nurses interrupting every two hours to check Brian's vitals, I felt like I looked. Fortunately, Brian slept through most of the poking and prodding.

With no toothbrush or comb and rumpled clothes, I resembled a before picture. Combing my hair down with my fingers, I was embarrassed to stand before Brian's doctor when he explained the care of his arm cast. After a follow-up appointment was made for the cast removal in eight weeks, we were to wait for our discharge papers.

Brian, with seemingly no worries, was more interested in the lunch tray and enjoying the multiple cable channels on the television than leaving. This made me realize how isolated the farm could be from the rest of the world. I just wanted to get out of there.

It took them several hours to get him discharged.

By the time we arrived back at the farm, it was late afternoon. Brian went to his room to rest. The excitement of the last day's events must have caught up to him.

At supper time, Betsy prepared Brian a tray. As she started up the stairs with it, I followed closely behind her.

When we entered his room, Brian propped himself up in the bed with his pillows.

"Now, that's a pretty sight, two of my favorite women toting a tray of goodies," he said, looking refreshed from his ordeal.

"Are you in any pain?" I asked.

"It just aches a little," he responded holding the arm up. Upon seeing the food, he said, "Oooh, my favorites." He winked at Betsy as she settled the tray on his lap.

"I'm just so glad you are okay." Betsy gushed as Brian dug into his roast and red potatoes.

"Don't ever scare me like this again." She shook her finger at him.

"Yes, ma'am," he responded, "I've learned my lesson."

Betsy fussed with his covers and cut on the overhead fan to cool the room. Standing in the doorway, she turned with glistening tears in her eyes, she said with a British lilt. "I'm really ever so glad you're okay, really, I am." She went down the hallway, leaving the door cracked.

I pulled the wing chair from the corner of the room to his bedside. "There's lots to look at in here," I said, nodding to the wallpaper covered in so many species of birds.

"I really like the bird room," said Brian. "It's like being in the woods, among the trees. "After a long day of working the fields, or with the cattle, I lie here, memorizing them. It's like I can almost hear them singing," he joked.

I nodded and smiled at his youthful enthusiasm.

"So." I paused. "We need to have a conversation about what you want to do at the end of the summer." I sat forward to gauge his reaction.

"I can't go back to the house. That woman is there, and Dad is weird, always on me. Can't I just stay here? I really like Gil and he says the high school here has a vocational agricultural program. I already know I'm good at that kind of thing and I like what I'm doing." His forehead wrinkled with concern.

"Look," he said, adjusting his tray. "I'm sorry for dad, I am. But I'm not a kid anymore. I feel like a man doing this kind of work, and it's what I want if that counts for anything."

"Finding you can make a living at something you like doing, that's everything," I answered with relief, feeling justified. It could be that I had made the right decision in bringing us to the farm.

Jake is going to go ballistic. I have another mountain to climb, *geesh*.

After a few days of Betsy's pampering, Brian was getting anxious to get back to work. He was planning his return, figuring out ways to manage two-handed chores with his one good arm.

We were all spoiling him, even Cindy. She would go into his room at night after everyone was in bed. I could hear her talking to him. I imagine her telling him about her day and catching him up on what was going on around the farm. These two were never close. As they were growing up, Cindy had very few friends, but they were a tight knit group. Brian had his sports and made friends easily. They seemed to have more in common now. It made my heart beat with happiness to hear them laughing together. My children like each other! I wish I could make out what they are saying. If I were to be discovered with my ear pressed up to the door, I might jinx the whole thing.

As the slow summer days came one after the other, we all had our jobs to do. A drought had settled in and seemed like it was here to stay. We were irrigating most days to keep the ground from becoming packed and cracking. Our saving grace was the greenhouses. If our yield from the fields didn't pan out, the plants and produce from the greenhouses would carry us through to fall. The controlled environment was expensive to operate but necessary. We may need to look into solar power to run the fans. Electricity isn't cheap.

The sun had begun to set, and I still had my meeting with Ranger to conclude my day. Grabbing my tablet from the office, I headed to find Ranger. He was waiting for me in the kitchen.

Betsy and Aunt Millie had been canning tomatoes all day and cooking food for the Church's Homecoming tomorrow.

The kitchen was surrounded by mason jars, shiny and full of red tomatoes. Every flat surface was covered. There was an occasional popping sound, indicating that the lids were sealed. I love that sound.

Ranger was leaning against the sink with a dish towel over his shoulder. Apparently Betsy had wrangled him into clean up duty. The room looked smaller with this large man standing in it.

"Sorry to keep you waiting. Are you ready for our meeting?" I asked him.

"Ladies, it's been a pleasure." Ranger bowed as he handed his dish towel to Aunt Millie.

"Let's go out to the porch," I suggested. "It's stifling hot in the office."

We settled on the east corner, away from the last rays of the sun sinking in the west.

Sitting at the table, I powered up my tablet and went over what had been done that week. We ran off a checklist of needs for each field. Fortunately, we would be able to harvest most of our corn and melons very soon. Our next step would be to prepare the fields for fall crops. Our pumpkin patch was already started. It would need a lot of attention in the coming weeks. If we didn't get rain soon, it might not have much of a chance.

In the greenhouses, cucumbers, zucchini, and Brussels sprouts were almost completed.

We were ready to convert to early fall vegetables, similar to what was grown in the spring. We already had our starts for cabbages and onions. The folks that run our booth at the open market in town were already asking if those would be available soon.

Ranger seemed a little on edge. "Are you worried about the weather, or is there something else on your mind?" I asked.

He sat back in his chair, causing it to creak slightly. Looking up, he seemed to be studying the tops of the trees. "It's this homecoming thing at the church tomorrow. Not a big fan of crowds, but I feel obligated to go," he said, studying my face.

Remembering something Aunt Millie told me, I didn't press him further. When I first started managing the farm, she advised me to not push Ranger on personal matters. Ranger, being the best foreman she had ever had, was a private person.

His stare was so intense, time stood still. Was he protecting me from something? What's with the look? Mystery!

I continued on as if nothing had just happened between us. "So, our trees. Do you think they will be big enough by Christmas?" We had perhaps foolishly started an evergreen venture for bringing in funds during the winter lull.

"Pray for rain," was his response.

"I guess that's about it tonight, for me. Do you have anything else that needs attention?"

"We are losing a couple of our hands this fall. Young Preston is starting agriculture classes at UT, and Bob is getting to the age of adulthood where he wants to start his own spread. With the season winding down, we won't be shorthanded. I still have a couple of men that we can hire from their farms part time if need be. And I expect that Brian will be healed and able to help after school hours and weekends."

"Thank you. It's a relief to have someone with experience. This is my first rodeo," I laughed. "I'd be lost without your help." I involuntarily blushed. Why am I blushing? How embarrassing.

Ranger looked amused. "Well, I guess I'd call it a night," he said, standing and replacing his chair under the table.

"Night" we said at the same time, in harmony. It surprised us both. We laughed.

He ambled toward the bunk house. He would be up before the sun, checking on everything. Some would argue about what the definition of a real man is, but I think Ranger would come as close as you could get.

Chapter 24

Coming down the stairs on Sunday morning, I find Brian dressed for church and sitting at the table over a plate of ham and eggs. His shirt was buttoned crookedly, but other than that, he looked ready to roll. Tucked into one end of his cast was an ink pen.

"What's with the pen?" I asked. "Is it for scratching the itchiness?"

"Nope, got to get this baby signed," he grinned, holding up the cast.

"Maybe put it in your pocket, instead. I'd hate to see the inside fill with ink if the pen were to leak or break open." I gave him my mom look.

"Yes, ma'am." He slid the pen out and put it in his pocket, noticing his shirt was buttoned wrong. "Um, would you mind fixing my shirt before the guys come in?" His eyes pleaded.

"Of course. Wouldn't want them seeing that." I smiled at him.

We unbuttoned, straightened, and buttoned again, bringing me back to a memory of dressing him when he was a squirmy little boy.

"Hadn't done that in a long time," I murmured quietly to him.

"Let's hope you never need to again," he joked.

Cindy came bounding down the stairs in her summer gingham dress with her long, honey-colored hair up in a bun.

"You look nice." I smiled at her.

"Thanks," she responded, running to the door to look out toward the bunk house. Then, her face fell.

I stepped over to look out and noticed that Ranger and the hands had already left.

"Guess we are getting a late start today." Curiosity at her behavior whirled around inside my head.

The door opened as Betsy and Aunt Millie came inside from the porch where they were having their usual morning cup of coffee, an event that happened each day but didn't include me. I'm not jealous, much. Both of them were ready for church with open dressy sandals and shirtwaist dresses of blue and green. I felt plain standing next to these three in my brown sandals and pale, yellow dress. It doesn't matter. All the people I love are here, together, going to church. Happy day.

Taking Aunt Millie's sedan, we arrived at the church with a few minutes to spare. It was Homecoming Day, a celebration for when Clover Dell Missionary Church was established in 1936. Members brought their extended family, and former members came back to get reacquainted with old friends.

Parking was difficult. The small asphalt parking lot was full. Cars and trucks were lined up both ways on the side of the road.

I dropped Aunt Millie and Brian at the church's front door and pulled up to the fellowship hall. Betsy and Cindy helped me take our covered dishes into the kitchen for the dinner on the ground that would take place after the preaching and singing. As I stopped to open the door to the kitchen, Cindy bumped into me with Aunt Millie's Pyrex dish full of meat loaf.

"Whoa, distracted much?" I asked.

"Sorry," she said, checking the back of my dress. "You're okay."

Moving some things around on the buffet table, we found spots for our dishes.

While Betsy and Cindy went into the church, I drove down the road and parked the car as far off the side as I could. The walk back into the church had me sweating by the time I got there. I should have put my hair up in a bun like Cindy did. It was sticking to the back of my neck. Thank goodness there is air conditioning inside the church.

Ranger and Bond Winston were talking off to the side in front of a grave marker. I slowed my pace, reading the name on the marker:

Sheena J. Clark-Adams
Beloved Wife and Sister

They both looked up at me as I passed. Bond's eyes were heavy and sad. Ranger's were dark, stormy. I gave them a little wave. Bond tipped his head up in greeting, looking more handsome than anyone has a right to. Ranger looked at the ground, his Stetson hiding his face.

I stepped as quietly inside the church as I could and was relieved by the rush of cool air. Goose pimples rose on my arms. I suppose it was the sudden change in temperature. Or maybe it was what I saw in the entryway.

Cindy was standing next to one of the hands, talking close, too close. Which one was he? Preston Powell, yes, that's his name. He's from Kentucky, Lexington, I think. He's the one headed to UT this fall.

Upon seeing me, they stepped back from each other, turned and went inside to sit on opposite sides of the back pews. He must be why she was so interested in what was going on at the bunk house this morning.

Oh, boy. Lots of mysteries to solve.

Spotting Betsy and Aunt Millie, I slide in between them. They had saved a space for me. It was a full house. My parents were there; I hadn't anticipated that.

They were sitting opposite each other, with my father on the front pew and my mother with the older ladies on the second pew from the front. He looked all business. She looked buttoned up. Aunt Millie patted my arm with assurance. Craning my neck, I searched for Brian. He and Gil were in the back corner with the Clarks and the Andersons. Meagan and Cindy, sitting next to each other, were talking and looking over at the boys.

A vague memory of being that age with my cousins and their friends came to me. We girls were just like that over Bond and his running buddies. History repeats itself once again.

Trying to pay attention to the sermon was next to impossible. Questions and anxious thoughts were pinging back and forth in my mind.

Who is Sheena? Is she Ranger's sister, wife, mother? How is she related to the Clarks? What kind of bombarding will I be getting during the meal from my parents? How serious is Cindy about Preston?

After the completion of the sermon and invitational hymn, the pastor extended an invite for what he called the best vittles you'll ever put in your mouth. Laughter rippled through the congregation as people stood and began talking with each other.

I leaned into Aunt Millie, "Who is Sheena Clark Adams?" I asked.

Her eyes widened, "Oh, what a tale of woe." She shook her head. "She was Jim Clark's little sister. She and Ranger were married for about seven years when she went for a joy ride with Bond Winston and they had an accident, rounded a curve and met a tractor head on. They went off the road and hit a tree. Sheena didn't survive her injuries and Bond had only minor ones. Everyone speculated as to why she would be in his car." Aunt Millie paused and looked around to see if anyone was within ear shot. "Bond never misses an opportunity to, um," she cleared her throat, "take advantage of a situation." She looked at me over her glasses. "If you know what I mean. That's why there's bad blood between him and Ranger, and rightly so!"

"Oh," was all I could think to say. Looking around the sanctuary, I didn't see Ranger or Bond. It's going to be hard to pretend I don't know these things. I almost regret asking.

As we stepped outside, my mother came up beside me with my father in her wake. The sun was blinding, and I shielded my eyes to look at her. A slight breeze had picked up, but it wasn't moving her updo hair. It wouldn't dare! My father offered his arm to help her down the stairs. When we reached the bottom, she turned to me. "You know, Ann, God hates divorce." She pursed her lips. I am such a disappointment to her.

"He hates adultery more." I squared my shoulders. "It's in the top ten."

She gave me a "hahrump" sound with a look of condensation. "Let's go eat, Daniel!" she ordered my father.

"I'll be right with you," he responded, guiding her away from me. We watched her teeter across the pavement toward the picnic tables in her sling-back high heels.

"I'm sorry," he said, sounding sincere. "She has her convictions, and nothing will change them. Please don't think too harshly about her. She has difficulty seeing you make choices that cause you hardship. Also, she is easily embarrassed." He shrugged. "To be completely honest, which I think is important, your mother gets a lot of ribbing by some of the female members at our church. They are competitive about the success of their children. She hasn't had a lot to brag about lately."

"My bad, Dad," I said defiantly. "Maybe if the two of you cared more about what's happening to me than how things look to others, I would have had enough confidence in myself to not make bad choices." Turning away from the sun, I looked him in the eye.

My anger, making me brave, I stood as tall as possible. "I wasn't loved at home. So, the first guy that showed me love was a lifeline. His love wasn't genuine, and I suffered for it, for years. He gave himself to someone else. Do you really think I should have stayed in that, honestly?"

He took his handkerchief out of his back pocket. It was such a familiar gesture. He wiped his brow. "I can't discuss these things with your mother. She becomes so upset. But I'm hoping you did the right thing. Are you planning to continue running your aunt's farm? What does your future look like?"

Without divulging Aunt Millie's condition, I replied, "Yes, I think I have found something I'm good at, and I plan to make a go of it. So, Mother can tell all her cronies that her daughter is successfully managing the family farm."

Just at that moment, Bond came up behind me. "Hey, pretty lady, Pastor Hopson." He nodded at my father. "There's lots of great food. Let's get something to eat." He cupped my elbow.

My father took a step back and looked at me with curiosity.

Not looking back at Bond, I looked at my father and answered, "No thanks, I've lost my appetite."

Pulling my arm away from Bond, I walked away from both of them toward the graveyard.

Finding shelter under a shade tree in the north corner, I sat down on the ground, not caring if my yellow dress became grass stained.

Looking toward the fellowship hall, I could see people mingling and eating at the picnic tables. Across the road, the ice truck was parked with its colorful awning. Kids were already lined up for snow cones. Since childhood, I remember the same man coming every year. I wonder what he does the rest of the year. He probably sells at county fairs and school functions.

Ranger was in line. I watched as he purchased one cherry and one grape. Surprisingly, he headed my way. Side stepping headstones, he gingerly made his way through the graveyard. As he settled beside me, I could hear his knees popping. He avoided eye contact.

"Cherry or grape?" he offered, extending the snow cones that looked small in his strong, dark-skinned hands.

"Cherry," I answered.

Silently, we sat slurping on our icy concoctions. It was peaceful. Sometimes saying nothing says so much.

We sat like that until my hinny was feeling numb. I stood to stretch, and he did likewise.

"You're doing a good job. Don't let nobody tell you differently," Ranger said, breaking the silence.

Looking into his big, soulful eyes, I said softly, "Thank you. I needed that."

He took my empty paper sleeve, stained red from the snow cone. Adjusting his hat with the other hand, he ambled through the graveyard towards the road. After discarding our paper cones in the trash can, he climbed in his truck and headed back toward the farm.

Most people had finished eating and were gathering up dishes and clearing away plates.

The teenagers had started a volleyball game in the field behind the fellowship hall. They didn't have a net or any boundaries but were having a fun time, the girls squealing and the boys showing off their muscles.

Brushing grass and leaves from the back of my dress, I headed toward the tables to help with cleaning and packing up food. I just wanted to go home.

Chapter 25

The heat was too much for Aunt Millie's old Buick's air conditioner. A strange mist began pumping out of the air vents. Our only choice was to drive home with all four windows down. We were wilted from the day's activities.

Cindy's bun was loosened, and strands of hair were flying around her head. Aunt Millie was fanning and dabbing her face with tissues. Betsy, head laid back, eyes closed, was resting herself. Brian was riding shotgun, admiring the signatures on his cast. Me, I had my eye on the odd-looking sky.

Dark clouds were coming in fast from the west. I hoped to make it to the house and unload the car before the sky opened up, although a cool drenching would be welcome. My legs were sticking to the vinyl seat.

As we rounded the curve just before the cut off to our driveway, sprinkles started to pelt the windshield. By the time we got our windows rolled up, we were hit with a wall of water. As we topped the hill, the deluge was so hard we could barely make out the shape of the house. The trees, lining the driveway, were bending and weaving in the wind. Lighting flashed, temporarily blinding me. I slowed the car to a roll. Pulling into the shelter of the carport, we were still being hit with rain blowing sideways.

"Well, we could make a dash for it, or sit here and wait it out," suggested Aunt Millie.

"Hey, look!" Brian shouted. "It's Dad." He pointed to the porch.

Sure enough, huddled in a chair next to the front door, Jake was getting wet. I rubbed a hole with my fist on the steamed windshield to see him better. Lightning flashed. We counted Mississippi's until the thunder roared. We only got to two. It was right on top of us.

"We sit tight." I insisted. "No need to get zapped with lightning." What is he doing here?

"Jake is the one in trouble. That can't be safe, sitting out there in the open," said Betsy, just as lightning flashed again. We could smell the electricity.

Serves him right, I could just imagine the headline: "Cheating Spouses Take Heed, Beware of God's Wrath!"

Our count, following the booming thunder, proved that the storm was moving away from us. After sitting for five more minutes, we all agreed to head for the door. Unloading the things from the car will have to wait until the storm passed.

Staying close against the house, the five of us side-stepped to the front door.

Brian, getting there first, greeted his father, "Hey, Dad."

We all huddled close to the house as Aunt Millie unlocked the door. I couldn't help thinking there was a time we didn't lock the door. No longer.

Bringing up the rear, I held the door for Jake. "Go on in!" I shouted over the storm.

He looked terrible, unshaven, clothes rumpled, red-eyed and wet. He hesitantly complied.

Betsy and Aunt Millie, giggling like schoolgirls, removed and cleaned their wet glasses using the kitchen dish towel. Occasionally, they stole a glance in our direction, the four Cantrell family members, soaked, curious, broken, and waiting for an explanation from their former leader.

"Dad?" Cindy's raised eyebrows asked everything with her expression.

"I'm," he started. Cupping his hands over his face, he said, "I'm so sorry. So, so, so, very sorry for what I did to our family. I've been a fool. It's all on me, I messed up everything for all of us."

Lowering his hands, he looked pleadingly at us. "Can you ever forgive me?"

No one moved. It was as if we were frozen in an awkward position.

A clear thought came through the fog in my mind. "Shirley left you, didn't she?"

He looked at me, a storm in his eyes, like the raging one outside. He nodded yes.

"Let me guess, greener pastures?" I asked sarcastically. I'm not making this easy for him.

Again, he nodded.

"She's on her way to busting up another family. This one has old money, wealth that can buy her trips to Europe." He looked ashamed.

Ranger poked his head in the door. "Everyone safe in here?" he asked, looking around the room, rain dripped from his hat. Sizing up Jake, he removed his rain slicker and hat, leaving them outside.

Folding his arms across his chest, he stepped toward Jake. "I don't believe I've had the pleasure."

"Ranger Adams, Jake Cantrell." I introduced them. "Ranger is our foreman," I explained to Jake.

Jake looked up at Ranger, then over at me. I could see the wheels turning inside his head.

"Good to meet you," Ranger responded, extending his hand. They shook hands briefly.

"I'm guessing that is your truck out there, being that Cantrell Construction is written on the side." He nodded his head toward the door, his black hair gleaming with the movement.

"Yes, I have . . . *had* . . . a construction business," Jake answered, standing a little taller.

"Had?" Brian and I asked at the same time.

"Yes, about that, could we speak in private?" He directed toward me.

"Not sure I'm comfortable with that." I stepped back. "Let's just have a seat here on the couch, and you tell us all about the adventures of Jake and Shirley." I pulled Cindy and Brian to sit on either side of me on the sofa.

Jake, reluctantly, sat in Aunt Millie's recliner in front of us.

A blinding bolt of lightning was followed by earth shattering thunder. The house windows rattled, and the lights flickered. I was so glad to have everyone inside the house safe and that Ranger was in the room. He respect-fully moved into the kitchen to stand against the wall with Aunt Millie and Betsy seated at the table. We were all ears.

Jake, sitting anxiously on the edge of his seat, put his hands together like he was praying and began. "I took out a loan against the business to keep Shirley in the lifestyle she wanted." Embarrassment made his face go red. "I took out a second mortgage on the house, so, I am now upside down on it."

"What does that mean?" asked Brian anxiously, his voice cracking.

"It means, he owes more than the house is worth on the market." I pat-ted his leg to assure him.

"After she left, I found a great amount of credit card debt and real-ized she had taken money from the savings. Basically, she wiped me out. I couldn't cover payroll for my crews. So, they left to work for other contrac-tors. I'm left with a mountain of debt, and the only way I can recover is to sell the house. It won't take care of all of the debt, but it will make it some-what manageable." He sat back, drained.

My mind drifted to the story of the lion with a thorn in its paw. If I remember correctly, a little mouse pulled it out for him. I can't remember if the lion was so grateful that they became friends for life or if the lion ate the mouse because he was a lion. Maybe I'm thinking of the snake that, after bit-ing its rescuer, said, "You knew I was a snake when you took me in." Shaking my head, I try to focus on Cindy and Brian's reaction to this information.

They stared at their father. Cindy broke the silence with a small chuckle. "Karma."

Brian looked over at her, then at his father. "What makes you think any of this has anything to do with us?"

"Well, that was your home." Jake looked defeated. "I thought you'd like to know what's going on." He shrugged.

"We've made our own plans," Cindy said flatly.

"Yeah, this is our life now." Brian raised his arms, his cast just missing my head.

"I'm sorry for your troubles, Jake," I told him. "But the world keeps turning. We are all building a life for ourselves. Cindy and Brian have blos-somed here. They like the country life and are planning their futures around it. Brian wants to start school here in the fall. He has made new friends and knows what he wants to do. Cindy has plans for college. Your children have grown up. They are making their own decisions." I paused and stood.

"I guess we should be thanking you. If you hadn't been an absentee spouse, if our family hadn't been broken, I wouldn't have moved out. The three of us are in a better place than we were just this time last year, thanks to Aunt Millie and Betsy." Looking at them sitting at the table, my heart felt warm.

Ranger looked like a statue, protective and silent. Betsy's eyes were glistening. Aunt Millie clasped her hands together and concentrated on the tabletop. I could tell she was calming herself. All this excitement can't be good for her heart.

"How can we help, Jake?" I asked in hopes of resolving and ending this meeting.

"I guess I just need forgiveness. I'd like to make things up to each of you. Maybe have a chance to try again."

Leaning toward me, he whispered, "I'd like to know that it's not too late for us." He motioned to me with a finger.

"Jake! We are divorced, there is no us! This is my life now." I pointed to the floor. "Could you really imagine yourself living on a farm?" I folded my arms in defiance.

His eyes went dark. He set his jaw. "The house is going on the market. I will be living at the business for a bit until I can get back on my feet. I need to know that I still have my family," he said as he stood up. His expression had turned into a pout.

So, once again, it is about him and what he needs.

Cindy and Brian stood with him. He hugged each of them with a long embrace. "Thank you for hearing me out," he said to all of us, his eyes sending daggers my way.

As he stepped outside, Cindy and Brian followed him. I watched him through the door signing Brain's cast as Cindy looked at the porch floor.

They had another hug, a group one this time. Jake made a run for his truck, giving them a toot with his horn before heading off as the rain pelted, dimming the sound.

Cindy and Brain stood on the porch, talking for what seemed like an eternity before coming back inside. Without a word or a glance, they both headed upstairs.

Betsy jumped up from her seat. "I'll make us all a good cup of coffee. It's been too hot for it lately, but I think it's just what we need right now."

I am so grateful for her. She's like a ray of sunshine on a cloudy day.

She and I have decisions to make, too. I'm going to need to sell or rent my condo. That money will help Cindy with tuition and books. Now that Jake hasn't the means, it's completely up to me to provide for our daughter. I love the way she said "karma." That's my girl.

Chapter 26

Monday morning was crisp and clear. The air had a freshness that made you think of renewal and hope.

Commodore and I had an early morning ride in the cool air. We watched the sun begin to rise as I gave him an extra-long brushing. He and I are becoming very good friends.

Coming into the mud room, I removed my boots and washed my hands. The hand towel at the sink smelled sour. I tossed it in the clothes hamper and got a clean one from the cabinet. It's laundry day. A load was already agitating in the washing machine.

Hanging my straw hat on the hook, I enter the kitchen in socks and stepped in something wet and warm. The kitchen sink was overflowing. I turned off the tap and opened the drain to let some of the water out. Going back into the mud room, I stripped off my wet socks and put them in the hamper.

Pulling the mop from its closet, I began mopping up the floor. When I had finished, I make my way to the office. Betsy almost collided with me in the hallway.

"The dishes!" she shouted.

"You're okay," I stopped her. "But be careful when you go in the kitchen. The floor is still wet."

"Oh, I'm so sorry. I got distracted getting the sheets from Millie's bed and forgot I'd left the water running. Those are the dishes from yesterday. They needed soaking. I don't know where my mind is today. I guess I was in la la land." She twirled her fingers in little circles around her head.

Following her to Aunt Millie's room, I helped her finish removing the sheets.

"There's something I wanted to talk to you about," I started. "It looks like I'm going to be staying here permanently. I was thinking I'd sell or rent my condo. That will get me out from under that monthly payment, and I will be able to help Cindy with her tuition for school this fall." I look at her judging her response.

"Has Cindy spoken to you lately? She may have other plans." She hesitated. "Maybe you should talk with her." She pursed her lips. "Also, the HOA won't allow renting the condo. It's in the contract," she said with a business tone.

Swooping up the bundle of sheets, Betsy headed out the door.

I began my search for Cindy, wondering what was going on. She wasn't in her bedroom. Brian, slipping passed me in the hallway, called over his shoulder, "Off to learn about shearing sheep."

"Well, that's something you don't hear every day," I replied. "Wouldn't happen to know where your sister is this morning, would you?" I asked.

"Nah," he responded, eyes darting away from me, bounding down the stairs.

"Get something to eat before you go!" I shouted to his back. What does everyone else seem to know that I don't know?

Stepping outside, I located Aunt Millie on the back porch, breaking beans in her lap.

I had a lot of work waiting for me in the office but knew I wouldn't be able to concentrate. "Good morning," I greeted her.

"Good morning, dear girl. How's my favorite niece this morning?" she chirped.

"I'm curious," I answered.

Reaching in her gathering bucket, she handed me two scoops of beans.

Using my foot, I pulled a chair over and sat, laying the beans in my lap.

Stripping each side of the beans and breaking off the ends, I dropped them in her discard pile. The beans popped as I snapped them into bite size pieces. They had a wonderful smell. This beats sitting behind a computer any day. Looking at Aunt Millie's hands, I can see how they have aged, bent and swollen around the knuckles. She's still the expert, breaking the beans much faster than I can.

"Did Cindy say where she was off to this morning?" I asked between the snaps.

"I believe she and that feller Preston were going to see about the damage from the storm last night. She said something about the greenhouse covering being loose." Aunt Millie looked a little smug, like a cat that had swallowed a canary.

"Why is it that I feel I'm being left out of something?" I teased her.

She shrugged and grinned.

"Sure was an interesting event yesterday," she commented.

I could tell she was testing the waters.

"Interesting is a good word for it," I responded, grabbing another scoop of beans.

"Well," started Aunt Millie. "I've of two minds on the matter." She talked as she worked. "What Jake did was horrific. Some would say, unforgivable. He does deserve to suffer. But forgiveness would be beneficial for you and the children. It's like releasing the hurt, setting yourself free from the situation." She looked up at me with tenderness.

Taking a deep breath, I released it slowly. "I've been so busy learning about running the farm and keeping things going. I hadn't really sat down and thought about him much at all. I guess the only exception would be a question of what his role in Cindy and Brian's life might be now."

"I guess you didn't pick up on the fact that he wasn't just talking about getting them back. He meant you as well." Her eyebrows raised.

"No, I don't think so." I shook my head. Not going to happen! "Things were not good with us for so long. Even if there hadn't been a Shirley, we were not going to make it. There's no reason to think we would now. I couldn't go back to that, just couldn't," I insisted.

"I understand," she nodded. "I think he might not. You know how men can be, need to see things for themselves."

We finished breaking the beans. As Aunt Millie took her basket into the house for canning, I dumped the scraps on the compost heap. The heat was building; it was going to be another scorcher today. My office work awaited me.

I powered up my computer. I have more than thirty emails to answer, supply bills to pay, and a few phone calls to make. Might as well get started.

After working for several hours, my stomach began to growl. I remembered that I hadn't eaten any breakfast. I make my way to the kitchen and helped myself to a blueberry muffin. Staring out the window over the kitchen sink, I noshed on the delicious muffin. Betsy is such a good cook. The canner was hissing and popping away on the stove. Shinny quart jars of beans sitting on clean towels were cooling on the kitchen table.

Betsy poked her head in the door. She was multitasking, doing laundry and canning beans simultaneously. "Are they boiling yet?" she asked.

Using a potholder, I tipped the lid enough to check. "Yep, just starting a good roll."

"Okay, thanks," she said, looking at the clock above the sink then disappearing around the corner.

Pouring myself a small glass of milk, I wash down the rest of my muffin. I felt the milk hit the bottom of my stomach, cold and filling.

Ranger's truck came into view. It was filled with broken branches from yesterday's storms. He and Preston proceeded to empty the load at the side of the woodshed. When given time to dry out, they would cut them up for firewood. Everything is used and nothing is wasted. I like the efficiency of that.

When they had finished stacking the branches, Ranger headed back toward the barn to park his truck, and Preston headed toward the greenhouses.

Cindy met him at the corner, sunlight bouncing off her golden hair. She smiled up at him.

He removed his working gloves and cupped her face. What happened next made me turn away from the window. That, my friends, was a kiss of two people in love. Oh, my.

I'm now reminded of Cindy's words from yesterday about having plans.

Could it be that Preston is a part of those plans?

The beans start to boil in earnest. Betsy came running into the kitchen with a basket of folded clothing. She plopped it down on the floor and tended to the beans.

"We need to talk," I said to her back. "What do you know concerning Cindy and Preston?"

"These beans, they look good, huh?" She smiled at me.

"Betsy, are you stalling?" I looked sideways at her. "Tell me what's happening with my daughter," I demanded.

"Ask her," she insisted. Her face relaxed. "If I talk to you about her, she may not confide in me ever again. Do you understand?"

Knowing Cindy, Betsy is right. She would see it as a betrayal if, after opening up to Betsy, her secrets were exposed.

Looking down at Betsy, I gave her my best smirk. "You're right."

She shrugged and shook her head. I could tell that she was struggling to hold her tongue.

As I head back to the office, I pray for the opportunity to talk to Cindy about her future and how this guy, Preston, just might be a part of it.

Chapter 27

Cindy and I had missed being in the same place the whole day. She wasn't at the table for lunch because of her life guarding job at the Anderson's campground. She had then stayed to have supper with Megan, according to Betsy.

Just before my head was about to hit the pillow, I heard her car coming up the drive. Listening for her footsteps in the hall, I opened the door just as she was passing.

"Hi," I greeted her startled face.

"Mom, you almost gave me a heart attack." She clutched her chest. Aunt Millie's heart condition flashed in my mind.

"Could we have a few minutes to talk?" I asked, hoping to not spook her any further.

"It's been a really long day." She rolled her eyes to emphasize how long it had been. "I just want to get out of this swimsuit and crash." She lowered her head to indicate her fatigue, then yawned.

"Go on then, get ready for bed and I'll come tuck you in, how's that sound?" I wasn't letting her off the hook. I needed to know what everyone else seemed to already know.

She reluctantly gave the slightest of nods with a heavy sigh. For just a flicker of a moment, I saw the old Cindy. It slipped across her face like a shadow, reminding me of so many fights from the past. Don't poke the bear.

Fortunately for me, she was too tired for a fight. After a long wait, I heard her leaving the bathroom. Giving her a few more minutes to get settled in her room, I mentally prepared myself for what could become a battle with the teenage mind.

I lightly rapped on her door, hoping that would show her my respect for her privacy.

She was cuddled up in her bed with the side table light on. She smelled so fresh. Her cheeks were glowing, with youthful vibrancy. My baby girl had become a young woman.

Risking rejection, I pushed her legs out of the way so that I could sit on the foot of her bed. She didn't object, adjusting her position.

Looking around the room, I study the sunflower wallpaper. The only wall, not papered is painted yellow. The metal frame bed sat against it with a sunflower painted in the center. Cindy hasn't put up any pictures or posters. The room looks much the same as it did when we first came to the farm. It's as if she hasn't really moved in.

Looking at her gently, I ask, "What are your plans for the end of summer? How can I help?"

Sitting up, she stacked her pillows against the headboard and leaned back and adjusted her sleeping T-shirt. Pulling the sheet across her lap, she smoothed out the creases.

Placing her hands flat, she stated, "I'm in love. Preston and I are engaged. We are starting to college this fall and will be living at Betsy's condo." She looked at me defiantly.

So many things went through my mind. You hardly know him. You're so young. Have you lost your mind? You've got to be kidding me! I hope she's not pregnant. Please, oh please, don't let my mistakes be repeated.

"Oh, Lord," I said with a groan.

I could tell that I had said the wrong thing by the cloud that came over her expression.

Regrouping, I steady myself. "When's the wedding?" I ask, nonchalantly.

"Labor Day weekend," she responded, her eyes going big.

I think I surprised her with my calmness.

"How can I help?" I asked gently.

She looked to the ceiling as if the answer were written there. Finding it, she said, "Help me tell Dad?"

"I can do that," I responded, dread creeping up my chest. "Give him a call, and we will go visit him after church tomorrow. Maybe we can all have lunch together somewhere. You can pick the restaurant."

She looked at her hands. "Okay." She nodded. Looking up at me, she said, "I'd like for Preston to come, too."

"Great," I said, hoping to sound enthusiastic rather than sarcastic. "We will make a day of it." I think I pulled it off. And the Oscar goes to...

Standing, I said, "Goodnight, sleep well, and congratulations."

Relief washed over her face. "Thanks, Mom. Goodnight."

Leaving her room, I closed the door softly behind me.

Walking in a stupor, I made my way outside to plop into the swing on the front porch. Gazing up at the night sky, I felt tears running down into my hair. My nose began to run. Seems I can't cry without my nose running. Wiping my face with my hands and my nose on my sleeve—I know, gross—I noticed lights still on in the barn.

I got up to investigate. As I got closer to toward the light, I hear Aunt Millie's voice, very low. She's talking to Commodore. He gently knickers as she rubs his nose. I slowly back out and give them their time together.

The air was so fresh and clean, I deeply inhaled. The smell of wet earth filled my head. Walking slowly back to the porch, I think back over how different our lives are and the huge change in my children. I feel so blessed. Now, my daughter wants to get married. I would be a true hypocrite to deny her wanting to make such an enormous move. Especially, since my decisions had catapulted us into our current situation.

When I got back to the porch, Ranger was waiting for me.

"Evening," he said in the night shadows. "Let's sit a minute."

I silently obeyed.

"Preston is a good young man," he started. "Do you have any questions or concerns regarding him?"

He sat with his long legs filling up the seat and his feet flat on the porch floor. I shifted in the swing, trying to get my tip toes to touch the boards. Giving up, I sat crossed legged.

"Seems like I'm the last to know about this romance. I'm trying to not take it personally. Tell me all about him. All I know is that Cindy has professed her love for him, and they are to be married come Labor Day weekend," I whispered in the dark.

"His folks are both schoolteachers. First generation college graduates. So, they want him to get a college education too. He would rather keep working here, training to step in when I retire. But being the obedient son that he is, he is going to study agriculture to appease his folks." He paused, waiting for my response.

"Retire?" I said a little too loud. Lowering my voice, I asked, "When do you plan to retire?"

He laughed softly. "I cannot do this forever. I've got maybe another decade of hard labor in me. I'm on just this side of fifty. It's time for the next generation to step in, use some of those fancy college ideas, really make this place come to life."

I mentally did the math of our age difference. Not too far apart.

He looked toward the barn. "Here comes Ms. Millie. Reckon she's done with her visit."

"You know about that? How often does she visit Commodore at night?"

"More these days. It's a little worrying. She seems to be slowing down more and more each day," he said with concern. "When I first come here in the '90s, I could hardly keep up with her."

He got up to assist Aunt Millie as she came up the porch stairs. I grabbed the chains to balance myself as the swing wiggled.

"Thank you, night all," Aunt Millie said out of breath.

"Night," we both responded. She went inside.

Ranger gently closed the door behind her. Putting his hands on his hips, he turned to look at me. "Seeing you sitting there, I can imagine what you looked like as a little girl."

"Hah!" I laughed. "Not even close. I was such a bean pole."

"Well, I will bid you goodnight unless there is anything else you wish to ask."

"What will you do when you retire? If you don't mind my asking. Do you have plans?"

"I've always wanted to see Alaska. I have people there. It is a welcome place for Native Americans. And I would love just to see it for myself." He looked off into the night sky as if he could see it in his mind.

"Alaska, the final frontier. It sounds ideal," I mused.

"If I don't see you in the morning, come Monday, the pumpkin patch needs attention. Fall will be on us before you know it." He tipped his hat and turned to walk to the bunk house.

Tomorrow is Sunday. Guess I'm having lunch with Jake, Cindy, and her intended. I'll think about that tomorrow.

Locking the front door behind me, I tiptoe to bed. The house is still but my heart is beating so loudly. So many thoughts are swimming in my head. A wedding, Jake's finances, my condo, getting Brian's cast off, Aunt Millie's health, Ranger retiring, summer ending . . . on and on go my thoughts like bees in a hive.

"Be still and know that I am God," I heard in my mind. Pulling up the covers, I feel more peaceful. "Thank you," I whisper to the ceiling and the heavens beyond.

Chapter 28

Sunday's church services were cut short. The air conditioning had stopped working, making the heat unbearable. With all the box fans going at full speed, it was still stifling. Aunt Millie, waving her paper fan, looked especially wan.

After taking her back home to her recliner and a glass of cold iced tea, I breathed a sigh of relief. She took a few sips, then pushed up her foot lift and nodded off into a nap.

Cindy and I prepared to head out for our lunch with Preston to meet Jake. Giving Betsy all the details, we left her to look after things until we returned.

After some discussion, we settled on taking Cindy's car. Preston, being gentlemanly, gave me the front passenger seat. He was trying to be on his best behavior. It was becoming awkward. We hadn't even left the property yet, and he had called me "ma'am" several times.

"Please, Preston, call me Ann." I insisted.

"Sorry, ma'am," he responded, his dark eyes shining. "My mother would have my hide. You're not just the parent of my fiancée, you're my boss as well." He vigorously shook his head no to deny my request.

I guess you can't take instilled manners out of a southerner.

We arrived at the Cracker Barrel a few minutes early. It wasn't crowded yet since most churches in the area were still having worship.

Preston got us a table under the name Cantrell so that it would be easy for Jake to find us. The host showed us to a table for four next to the window. We ordered our drinks and gazed around at all the antique memorabilia on the walls.

Cindy and Preston were easy with each other. I could see that they were very much in love. When Cindy talked, Preston listened intently and didn't interrupt her. Every so often, Cindy would blush. Her demeanor was lighthearted and upbeat. I hadn't seen her like this since she was a pre-teen having a sleepover with her friends. I wonder where those girls are now.

Rolling back the curtain of time, I pictured our home life. It was toxic. I concentrated on Jake's entrance after his long days on project work sites. If everything wasn't just so, dinner on the table, family fawning all over him, he would become angry. It wasn't long from that, the yelling would start. No wonder the children were reluctant to bring friends to their home.

"Penny for your thoughts," chimed Cindy, bringing me back to reality.

"Oh, sorry, I was off on a trip in my head," I apologized.

Cindy's cell phone made a cricket sound. Digging it out of her purse, her face dropped.

"It's a text from Dad." She frowned. "He can't make it."

Trying to keep things upbeat and not show my relief, I said a little too cheerfully, "Then, let's go ahead and order." I immediately felt guilty for not wanting to be in the same room with Jake.

Cindy gave me a look of disapproval, then shook it off. "Yes, let's order," she said evenly. Changing her mind, tears formed in her eyes. "Actually, can we just go?"

Preston, reading her pain, put his arm around her and comforted her. "Yes, we sure can," he said gently. Rising, he dropped a twenty-dollar bill on the table and assisted Cindy by pulling out her chair as she stood.

I took a long sip of my iced tea, told our waiter that we had to leave, and followed them out. Reaching the car, I insisted on taking the back seat. Without argument, Preston put Cindy in the front passenger seat. Sliding into the driver's position, he made sure everyone was buckled up before exiting the parking lot. Cindy rode home with her head on his shoulder most of the way.

I felt shame and embarrassment for this young man from a wholesome family to see our brokenness.

Arriving home, I was let out of the car. Preston and Cindy were going to continue their day together, alone. Cindy was staring a hole into the floorboard. Preston assured me that he would take good care of her. The walk into the house was slow and painful.

When I reached the front door, I could hear music. Someone was playing the Beach Boys' "Good Vibrations" at full volume. Opening the door, I find Betsy and Aunt Millie dancing with a broom and a mop. "Hi!" I yelled. "I need a partner."

Grabbing Aunt Millie's walking stick from the corner, I joined in the merriment. I had forgotten to keep dancing. The song ended and we fell onto the sofa, out of breath. I knew, tearfully, that this would be a moment I would reflect on for the rest of my life. To go from despair to joy in sixty seconds was certainly memorable.

Still breathing hard, Betsy asked, "How did it go?" Her eyebrows arched.

"It didn't," I answered flatly. "Jake was a no-show, and Cindy was so upset. But, on a good note, I really like Preston," I said with a lilt at the end.

"Figures, he's a coward," Betsy responded. "Not Preston, he's awesome. Jake, the snake." She made an ugly face and fangs with her fingers.

"Cindy was excited to have a meal with Preston and her family and tell her dad about her wedding. She was so disappointed, she had no appetite." I stood and went into the kitchen to stare in the refrigerator.

Spying some fried chicken, I pulled a leg out and started to nibble on it when my cell phone rang. It was Brian.

"Hey, Mom," said cheerful Brain.

It was his "I want something" voice. "Hey, Son," I played along.

"Gil's dog, Belle, had pups last spring, and they are now weaned, trained, and ready to be re-homed. I'd like to get one. Pleeeease," he pleaded.

"Hold on," I said, giving me a moment to think.

"Aunt Millie, Brian wants to get one of Gil's pups. What say you?" I put the ball in her court.

"Well." She rubbed her chin. "Them Border Collies do make awfully good cattle dogs. They're loyal too. I say, why not?" She shrugged. "It needs to be completely his responsibility."

Putting my phone back to my ear, I hear Brian rejoicing. Apparently he had heard his Great Aunt's answer.

"Okay, okay, Brian." I wait for him to calm down.

"Thanks, Mom." He sounded so grateful.

"Two questions," I started.

"Shoot," he responded.

"Boy or girl, and what's its name?" I asked.

"It's a boy, and we're going to name him Bill," he answered proudly.

"It's entirely your responsibility," I insisted.

"That's right," he answered, "because he is mine, all mine."

"Guess we're getting a dog," I announced to the room.

"Fantastic!" shouted Betsy, punching the air. "I've never had a dog, but I've always wanted one. Carl was allergic," she explained.

By suppertime, Brain came home with a ball of fur. Aunt Millie had never allowed an animal inside the house, but little Bill had wiggled his little fuzzy self into all our hearts. We took turns passing him around and talking sweet to him.

Brian, being in charge of his dog, scolded us. "You're going to ruin him," he insisted. "He's a trained herder, not a baby."

Reluctantly, we left the two of them alone so that Brian could take Bill out to the cattle and introduce him to his doggie duties.

We watched out the window as the duo bounded out into the yard. When Brian hopped onto his ATV, Bill jumped into the bucket seat on the back, and off they went to the cattle pasture.

"Well, if that isn't the sweetest thing I ever saw!" exclaimed Aunt Millie. She and Betsy were both standing with their fists clutched to their chest.

"I've got to admit it, that's pretty dang sweet," I said.

Preston and Cindy were parking as Brian pulled off. They all waved at each other. She looked much happier than she had earlier.

Coming into the house, Cindy announced, "I talked to Dad over the phone. After a bit of a meltdown, he has agreed to give me away. Preston asked him for my hand first." She clasped his hand and swung their arms together, beaming up at him.

Preston, blushing, said, "It was the proper thing to do," looking at Cindy adoringly.

Oh, brother, these two are going to give everybody diabetes with all this lovey-dovey syrup.

"Great!" I clapped my hands together. "So, I guess we have a wedding to plan, huh?"

"Well," hesitated Cindy. "We don't really want any fuss. The church is scheduled and the preacher. We want to keep things small." Looking at Preston, she waited for him to chime in.

"My parents are coming for that weekend; they are staying at the campground. Really, the only thing left to do is for everyone to get whatever they are going to wear together." He shrugged.

I just nodded. Betsy and Aunt Millie looked at me, sympathetically, knowing I was feeling pushed out.

With the telling of their plans settled, Preston and Cindy breezed back out to go for a sunset walk.

I excused myself and went to my room to cry and scream into my pillow. But it's all good, right?

Later, I heard a quiet tap on my door. "Don't want to talk to anybody," I called out. Whoever it was respected my wishes, leaving me be.

Chapter 29

The next few weeks were all about preparing for fall and Preston and Cindy's wedding on Labor Day weekend.

Gifts and invitation confirmations had begun to arrive. Our mail carrier started to drop off sacks instead of envelopes.

Ella Anderson and her daughter, Megan, were giving Cindy a bridal shower at the church fellowship room the coming weekend. All of the ladies of the church would be in attendance. According to Aunt Mille, this kind of thing is what they live for.

We were all relieved to have more favorable weather. Temperatures were milder and the rain was sporadic. We had more than enough hay for the winter. So much hay that we were able to sell the surplus with some time left in the growing season.

Seasonal beds were also thriving. The only worry was when the first frost would hit. It can come some years as early as October. If that should happen, we will harvest early and rely on the greenhouses for income.

We have big plans for the holidays with our Christmas tree fields, wreaths, and crafts already in the works. Ranger's efforts in growing the evergreens would pay off.

When I asked him how he kept the fields so clean of brush, he shrugged and said, "You bush hog everything else."

After getting approval from Aunt Millie, my gift for the lovebirds is a piece of land just over the rise. Their front porch view will be the Cumberland Gap, just above the lake and Anderson's campground. With a skip in my step, I picked up the deed at the County Court House last week. Not that I'm trying to buy their favor or anything like that.

As to her gift, Aunt Millie had her and Uncle John's wedding rings resized. Her eyes glowed with joy when she presented the rings to the happy couple. Cindy and Preston were honored and thrilled to have such a gift, hugging her with gratitude.

Betsy was all about recording their special day memories. She hired a band and photographer for the wedding. "Yes, there will be dancing at a Baptist church," she insisted.

As shy as Cindy is in front of people, Betsy might be dancing alone.

Cindy had her dress, a simple A-line made of crepe with a lace overlay. She didn't want a veil, just a hair comb with rhinestones. Her flowers were simple, too, pink tea roses tied with a white ribbon. Betsy is to be her matron of honor and Meagan her flower girl/maid of honor.

Preston asked Ranger to stand up for him and for Brain and Gil to usher. Brian was so happy to have his cast off and his new companion, Bill. He wasn't complaining about wearing an uncomfortable suit.

Aunt Millie, Betsy, and I are going to town this afternoon in search of dresses. I will probably wear something silver or gray. Betsy and Megan want to wear a soft pink, the color of Cindy's flowers; their bouquets are white as are the groomsmen's boutonnieres.

Ladies at the church are catering the food. Julia Clark, Gil's mother, is doing the wedding cake. Cindy loves carrot cake with cream cheese frosting. Preston just wants what Cindy wants.

On the drive to town, Aunt Millie wanted to make a stop at the hairdresser's. Coming back to the car, she beamed with success. "We all have an appointment next Saturday to get our hair and nails done for the wedding. Beatrice is coming in special just for us."

"Oh, how wonderful!" squealed Betsy from the back seat.

I couldn't help but roll my eyes. My head and nails hadn't seen a professional since I came to the farm. Beatrice is going to need a chisel and blow torch to whip me back into shape. Not to mention makeup—that makes me anxious. I don't want to look too made up. I'd like to be recognizable. "Does she do makeup too?" I asked hesitantly.

"No, not really. Just hair and nails," answered Aunt Millie. "Do you want makeup, too?"

"I think we can handle that, don't you?" I asked a little too defensively.

"You bet!" Betsy slapped the back of the seat. "It's going to be so much fun! Like a big ole party."

Arriving at the dress shop, I spot the dress I want in the window. It's a pale green, very feminine chiffon, tea length. I was so relived to find it in my size. Betsy found her soft pink, floor-length dress. It had a sash at the waist that she wasn't too pleased with. The sales lady said it was no problem to alter it. She would just remove the belt loops. Aunt Millie didn't see anything she liked until I pointed out a teal suit dress the same color as her eyes. After trying it on, she was sold.

I called Cindy at the farm to tell her we were staying in town, and she would need to take care of supper for the others.

"What?" she asked, shocked.

"You know, cook a meal for the hands, yourself, and your brother," I explained patiently.

"Any suggestions as to what I fix?" she asked anxiously.

"Honey, you're getting married. How do you expect to feed yourself and your husband? We've cooked together many times. Hopefully, you have picked up something along the way."

"I can't just call for pizza delivery, huh?" she asked flatly.

"Nope, figure it out. You can do it. This is good practice for you. Being married is figuring out every night what to fix for supper. It's his always being there and having to meet his needs too. It would give me great comfort to know you are ready." I waited her response.

After a long silence, she said a quiet, "Okay."

With that settled, our trio decided to get a meal at the diner while Betsy's dress was being altered.

Sliding into the booth where my children and I had eaten when we first came to the country, I was contemplative at all the changes since that time.

"Penny for your thoughts," said Aunt Millie.

"Sorry, I guess I'm daydreaming. So much has happened since the last time we ate here. Now, here we are with Cindy getting married. It's like a strange dream. I keep feeling like the other shoe is going to fall," I said, resting my head in my hands.

"Girl," Betsy growled. "You've had plenty of shoes fall. I don't think there is another one. Just be happy, enjoy. Viva de Vida loco!" She hopped up and did a slide step over to the juke box. Punching in her selection, Elvis came on with "Burning Love."

We had ourselves a sitting at the table dance, right there. Other diners joined in the fun at these three crazy ladies out on a Saturday night.

Chapter 30

Cindy and Preston's shower was a success. The only hiccup was a gag gift, which was probably from her brother, a dirty diaper. It wasn't real poop, but mud. Cindy tried to laugh it off, but you could see how angry and embarrassed she was by the flushing red spots on her neck. Brian and Gil, of course, thought it was hilarious.

The gifts ranged from cookware to linens. All were useful, and there weren't any repeats.

Seeing to polite etiquette, Aunt Mille had already helped Cindy prepare her thank you notes when making out the invitations.

Meagan, clipboard in hand, eagerly took the serious responsibility of recording the names of each giver and what gift they generously contributed to the marriage.

After refreshments were consumed and most party attendees had exited, we cleaned the fellowship hall, before strolling across the parking area to the church for the ceremony rehearsal.

Jake wasn't there to walk Cindy down the aisle. Since I wasn't a part of the wedding party, I stepped in to escort Cindy to her groom waiting at the altar with a huge smile on his face.

We followed Betsy, escorted by Ranger and Megan, escorted by Brian, down the aisle.

Stepping the wedding march, we paused at each step. "Last chance to run," I joked to Cindy.

"Mom!" she said in two syllables. "Really?"

When we completed the awkward walk, the pastor asked, "Who gives this bride in marriage?"

The answer was to be her mother and I. Which, the pastor answered for me, followed with his motion for me to have a seat.

From my front pew view, I could see Cindy's dress hem shaking. With all her vibrato of bravery, she is trembling with fear.

I drifted off into a daydream of the time that we had the talk. She was just starting sixth grade, and I explained the physical and emotional aspects of the facts of life to her. She had a few questions concerning her friends' information they had shared, which I was able to debunk without laughing. I left the door open for any other questions she might have, but with the exception of managing monthly protection, she hadn't asked for any other instructions. Hopefully, she would come to me or Betsy if the need should arise.

Looking to my right at Preston's parents on the front pew behind their son, I got a smile from his mother. They had arrived from Kentucky the night before and had supper at the farm before taking a cabin at the campground. Labor Day weekend was big business for the campgrounds. Fortunately, we had booked a cabin for them before the rush. They were very a down-to-earth couple and lighthearted in their conversation. I could tell the level of love and pride they had for their son. His mother, Melissa, who was—surprise, black—and his father, Mike, who was—surprise, white—were both warm and friendly. I was a little worried that some of the people of our community would be taken aback with Preston's parents being of different races. It was nothing for me to fret over. Everyone has treated them with nothing but respect. I especially liked Melissa. She knew so little of Cindy and felt left out of her son's life. We had an immediate connection, a common experience.

With both Mike and Melissa being teachers, lively discussions were the norm for them. They were interested in learning everything about the farm. Preston and Cindy were more than happy to give them a tour.

As the rehearsal was ending, Preston asked everyone to indulge him for one more moment. He had a gift for the bride. Reaching behind the pew where his parents were seated, he brought out package with a large blue bow.

Giggling and fingers shaking, Cindy began undoing the bow. "It's so pretty, I almost wish I didn't have to open it."

As Cindy opened the gift, Preston took the paper and bow from her. Cindy put her hand to her mouth, "Oh, Pres, it's beautiful." She then turned it around so we could all see. It was a photograph of them together, standing against the fence railing at the barn. Around the outside of the photograph was cross stitching with flowers and hearts and the words "You Are My Home" at the top and Cynthia and Preston and their wedding date at the bottom. "Wherever we live, this will hang on the wall," announced Preston.

Well, that just about had us all bawling our eyes out. Even tough-as-nails Ranger looked a little choked up. I wondered if he was thinking of his lost wife.

With the lights turned off and the doors to the church locked, we all headed home. Preston and Cindy left with Megan and his parents to the campground. Ranger and I headed back to the farm with all the shower presents filling the back of his truck. Betsy, Brian, and Aunt Millie tagged along behind us in the old Buick with Brian behind the wheel.

The shadows were long with the sun just setting. A hint of fall was in the air.

"I love this time of year," I said, breaking the silence.

"Yep," responded Ranger. "Football, bond fires, and changing leaves comes to mind."

"I'm going off memory of that seasonal change on the farm. Just like summer was, I'm learning as I go, but I look forward to the challenges. One thing I do dread is winter. I have a feeling it will be the hardest season of them all." I turned to check on the gifts in the truck bed, bows blowing in the wind.

"Winter is not so bad. Mostly it is preparing for the cold temps and weather. I have every faith that you can manage fine." Ranger nodded his head. "Maybe, just try to enjoy where you are for now."

"That's good advice." I relaxed back into the seat and let the breeze blow in my face.

Bill was waiting for us on the porch. He came bounding down to greet us.

Giving his head a good rub, I cooed at him, "You're a good boy."

As Brian pulled in, I was completely forgotten. Brian is his person.

We unloaded the wedding gifts and hauled them up to Cindy's room. Her dress was hanging on the curtain rod. It looked so soft and feminine. I wanted to touch it but felt like I should wash my hands first.

My baby is getting married. I can't think about that too much. I headed back downstairs, pushing away the urge to crawl in the bed and pull the covers over my head.

Ranger was standing next to the door. "Ms. Millie is headed to visit with Commodore. I have an idea and could use your help."

I shook a hard yes with my head, glad to have a distraction.

Brian was waiting on the porch with several coiled Christmas lights in his lap and Bill faithfully at his feet.

"We're going to string these up from the house to the barn. It's getting dark earlier, and Mrs. Millie might stumble on something." Ranger gave us our orders.

As he went to the shed for a couple of ladders, Brian and I got started going along the edge of the inside of the porch eave. Lights had been hung here every Christmas I could remember. The hooks were still in place.

Within about an hour, we had completed our task. Brian went inside the mud room and flipped the switch. A path to the barn was illuminated. There were a couple of bulbs that needed replaced, but what a difference a little light makes. I don't know why people don't leave lights up year-round.

We watched as Aunt Millie made her way back from the barn. She looked up at the lights and cupped her face like a surprised little girl. "Oh, how beautiful!"

Bill and Brian ran to her. Brian offered her his arm and escorted her the rest of the way.

My heart swelled with love.

I try to remind myself that I'm not losing one of my children tomorrow. I'm gaining a son-in-law and an extended family with his lovely parents. Just wish my heart knew that.

Chapter 31

Happy Wedding Day. The house is upside down. Everyone is rushing around to get ready for the Wedding. We were all waiting our turn to shower.

Betsy gave up waiting and went downstairs to Aunt Millie's bathroom.

After my turn with Beatrice doing the final touches to my hair and nails, I headed upstairs to finish dressing.

Cindy is eerily calm. She woke, stretching and yawning, smiling as if it were just another day. Passing me in the hallway, she greeted me with a cheerful, "Good morning, Mom. Isn't it a beautiful day?" Who is this person, and what has she done with my daughter?

I, on the other hand, was a nervous wreck. Not having worn make-up for some time, I kept smearing my mascara. I'm either out of practice or my hands are too shaky. Taking a deep breath and sitting on the edge of my bed, I try to settle my nerves.

Brian came to my door and knocked softly. "Come in," I answered.

"All the chores are caught up. I'm ready. So, I'm going to head on over to the church."

"Thank you," I answered with relief. "The florist and caterers should be set up. Would you mind checking that all is in order when you get there? I'll be driving Cindy over as soon as everyone is finished getting ready." He looked so handsome in his suit. "You look nice."

He looked at the floor. "Thanks, Mom. It's going to be weird not having her here, isn't it?"

"Yeah, it is." I nodded, fighting the emotions.

He stood up straighter and patted the back of my door. "Well, see you over there."

"Yep, see you there," I answered softly.

With one more look behind him as if he were about to say something else, he said nothing and headed down the hallway.

Standing, I smoothed out my pale green chiffon dress. Show time.

Making my way to Cindy's room, I hear Betsy call up the stairs that she and Aunt Millie are leaving with Ranger. Preston had stayed with his parents last night, so he would be getting them transported to the church.

I was honored that Cindy was going to let me drive her. Standing outside her door, I stilled myself and tapped lightly.

"It's open," she said.

Swinging the door open, I am met with a vision of a woman, her image soft and feminine. I noticed she is wearing the gold cross necklace I had given her at graduation. Her golden hair is pulled away from her face, held into a bun on the nape of her neck with Betsy's silver comb. Pale pink roses and baby's breath encircle the comb. Betsy probably did that. Her look will be completed when she gets her bouquet, matching the flowers in her hair.

"You are breathtaking, so beautiful." I smile at her.

"Thanks, let's do this." She smiles back.

On our journey to the church, Cindy talked about moving out and starting classes. She gave me a rundown of her plans to move into Betsy's condo and what she would need.

Since I'm putting it on the market, I offered her my furniture from my condo. She was pleased with that.

When we pulled into the parking area, Betsy met us with Cindy's bouquet. Preston was, fortunately, already inside.

A couple of attendees were making their way inside. The wedding party, congregating around my truck, waited until the coast was clear.

I heard Jake before I saw him. He was greeting everyone with pleasantries.

Cindy looked at me, nodding. She opened the truck door to start her new life.

The wedding procession began. I avoided Jake's presence. With my corsage pin poking me, I took Brian's offered arm and was escorted to the front pew. Preston's parents were already seated. They sparkled. Preston looked like a male model in his suit.

All the wedding party made it down the aisle as rehearsed. When the pastor asked who gives this woman in marriage, Jake answered, "I do."

Several gave him a look and then looked at me, but I let it drop.

He then proceeded to sit next to me. His cologne was smothering. I scooted away from him as much as I could.

The rest of the day was somewhat of blur. Jake was actually flirting with me, calling me Annie, saying how I clean up real good. It was like trying to shoo away a gnat. Then, here came Bond Wilson, asking me to dance.

I welcomed the interruption. He led me out on the floor to the *Dirty Dancing* song, "I Had the Time of My Life." Ranger, who was standing next to the punch bowl, stood up a little straighter and unfolded his arms, watching our every move.

Bond was holding me a little too tight; I pushed against his chest to make some space.

"Ah, now. Don't be that way," he cooed. "I bet we can do that famous lift at the end of the movie. Want to try?" he teased.

"When donkeys fly," I answered. "Thanks for the dance," I said sarcastically, removing myself from his embrace.

Spotting Betsy and Aunt Millie over in the corner table, I made my way to them. "Save me," I said, plopping down in a chair.

"I got you covered," Betsy announced. She intercepted Bond and pulled him onto the dance floor. The music had changed to a sweet country ballad. Betsy looked pretty with her soft pink dress flowing back and forth as she and Bond waltzed around the floor.

Cindy and Preston did their father, daughter, mother, son dance at the same time to the song "Butterfly Kisses." The bouquet and garter, her something blue, were both thrown. Bites of cake were exchanged. Then, before we were all quite ready, the bride and groom were leaving.

Preston shook hands with his father and kissed his mom. Cindy kissed and hugged everyone. We all blew bubbles at them as they climbed into Preston's truck and headed off to Gatlinburg for their honeymoon.

Suddenly, it was as if we were all deflated. Did we remember to put her suitcase in Preston's truck? Looking in my cab, I found it empty. Someone must have remembered to do that for her. I went back inside the fellowship hall, folks were clearing and cleaning. I began folding chairs. Within an hour, we had everything sorted and back in place. The photographer left me with a copy of the wedding pictures on a flash drive. I thanked everyone several times before putting the last bag of trash in my truck bed.

Jake, leaned up against my driver's door and cocked his head sideways, studying me. "It was some day, huh?" he asked, sincerely.

"Hard to believe our baby girl is a married lady, isn't it?" I said dusting my hands off.

"So." He stood up. "What you doing after?" He looked hopeful for a positive answer.

"Back to the house. I've a farm to run." I put my hands on my hips.

"That's too bad," he said, taking a step toward me. Touching my hair, he said. "We could have had some fun."

I stepped back. "Bye, Jake," I said, hoping he would just go away. "This," I motioned with my finger between us, "is never going to happen."

He put his hands in his pockets, jingling his keys as he slowly stepped away, walking backward.

I climbed in, slamming the door. Starting the engine, I pulled away, watching as he got smaller and smaller in my rear-view mirror.

I should have left sooner when everyone else did so he didn't have an opportunity to corner me. Well, I could kick myself all the way home. Or I could be proud that I didn't cave to his attentions. Maybe I'm really over him.

Saying a little prayer for Cindy and her husband, I rambled on home.

Chapter 32

We all got back into our routines on the farm. Aunt Millie instructed me as to what to expect with the harvest completed and winter prep on the horizon.

She seemed stronger these days, taking fewer naps and joining in on late-night board games and talks around the table of upcoming events.

Bond Winston had called a few times trying to get me to go to the movies or out to dinner. I got to where I'd take the message and not even return his calls. Can't the guy take a hint?

One evening, when we were moving the herd, I pushed Ranger to give me more information about the situation. He advised me to steer clear of that one. Ranger said that Bond goes through girls like a revolving door, omitting the history of his wife Sheena's demise. Answering Bond's next call, I shot him down. He finally took the hint and stopped trying.

A neighboring farm invited the community for a stir off, making molasses from sugar cane. It was to take place next weekend. Everyone was to bring a covered dish and take turns with the stirring. There was a prize of quart jars filled with the coveted brown liquid for everyone at the end of the evening.

Molasses had been the only sweetener before granulated sugar had made its way into the states. It was still a favorite. Aunt Millie always took one of her stack cakes, made from molasses, to the stir off. Betsy had a new chicken and dumplings recipe she wanted to try. Busy newlyweds and students, Cindy and Preston were coming and bringing a meat and cheese platter. There was always too much food. But we didn't care. It wasn't really about the food as much as it was about seeing everyone and spending time together.

Preston and Cindy had completely cleared out my condo. I brought the wicker furniture to the farm and plopped it down on the front porch. It looked like it belonged there. Aunt Millie made a claim on the rocking chair. She announced, "It fits my old bones to a T."

I hope it really was comfortable for her and she wasn't just being nice.

Betsy sold a lot of her things at the flea market. I stored what the kids didn't want from my things in plastic tubs in the back of the garden shed, dishes, linens, and the like. Who knows, Brian might want them when he ventures out into his future.

The real-estate agent I used to buy the condo took my listing. It was sold within two weeks of being on the market. Condominiums seem to be in high demand with all the baby boomers hitting retirement age. I was glad to have that monthly payment off my shoulders. Now, I could start putting my money toward projects at the farm. I'd like to rescue more horses for the programs that match up kids with disabilities with equine therapy.

The evening of the stir off, we arrived at the Roads End Farm, which was about five more miles down the road from our place. We need to give our farm a name. I'll have to talk to the troops about that.

At the Roads End Farm, Norris Lake bordered the northwest side, and there was a wonderful view of the Cumberland Gap. The Bailey family had run the farm for many generations.

The ladies all congregated in the kitchen, setting up tables covered with everyone's dishes. Brian carried Betsy's chicken and dumplings in for her. She was buzzing like a bee. This was her first stir off. She had been looking forward to this so much. She had been hard to live with all week, constantly asking questions of anyone that would answer her, wanting to know every detail of what this was going to be like.

The males of the community were tossing horseshoes. Ranger was among them. Some men were standing together over in the smoking corner, downwind side of the house, probably having political discussions. You could smell the smoke from the wood fires burning under the vat troughs where the molasses would be cooked down. Conversations close to that shed were almost drowned out by the tractor that turned the press squeezing sweet juices out of the sugar cane as it was fed through. Piled high on either side were wagons of fresh sugar cane and the discarded hulls. I must add here for our forefathers that, originally, mules were used to turn the press.

Some people had brought musical instruments and were huddled together on the porch, discussing what to play. One would begin a song that he or she knew, and the others would join in.

The children were running around the yard playing tag and giggling. Brian and Gil were keeping up with them. It was a scene right out of a Norman Rockwell painting. I couldn't help thinking, *This is the life.*

Cindy and Preston arrived just as dusk was settling in. Preston went to join with the workers at the cooking shed, helping with stoking the fire and taking turns stirring. Cindy went inside with her tray of meats and cheeses. Megan, ever her shadow, followed her inside.

I settled myself on the porch next to Ella Anderson. We sat there, content to watch the sun setting over the lake and listen to the music and laughter.

The musicians were playing "Tennessee Waltz" as Cindy came up to me. "Mom, could we take a walk? I need to talk to you about something."

Rising slowly, I looked at Ella. She was as clueless as I. "Sure," I answered. Megan plopped into my vacated seat next to her mom.

Cindy and I made our way toward the lake, high stepping here and there to avoid some mud. Large rocks lined the yard just before a slight drop down to the water. Cindy climbed up to sit on a flat one and patted the rock, indicating for me to sit beside her.

Pulling a large spray of overgrown grass, she proceeded to dismantle it, letting the seed heads be taken by the wind. Struggling to be patient, I waited for her to divulge the reason behind our solitary walk away from the activities.

"Mom," she started. "I'm pregnant." She looked sideways, gauging my reaction.

I closed my eyes. Took a breath. I was thinking, *Let my second reaction be my first.*

Looking at my daughter with compassion I ask, "When are you due?"

"End of May, maybe first of June," she answered, staring straight ahead as if she were in a trance.

"How can I help?" I felt joy swelling in my chest.

"Preston and I aren't really fitting in at college. We already know most of what is being taught. Matter of fact, Preston could probably teach some of the classes. We want to test out this semester and come back to the farm. Preston has big plans. He wants his child raised on the farm. He has ideas about starting a bed and breakfast with nature walks and horseback riding trails. Rather than having to work the land so hard, we would raise specific things to supply the B & B. He wants to get goats and make cheese with the milk. He has so many ideas. We both feel like we are just wasting money and time at college." She threw the remainders of her shredded grass stalk away and brushed off her lap.

"Well, if I have learned anything, it's how to start over," I answered.

Cindy leaned back and looked at me with a studying gaze. "When did you get to be so cool?"

"Hah!" I laughed. "I don't think I'm at all cool. But I have lots of practice at becoming more understanding. Oh, my, I'm to be a grandmother." Putting my hands on the side of my face, I made a silent screaming expression.

As we made our way back to the party, I couldn't help thinking that my girl has no idea how much work she has set herself up for. In my head I was already thinking up baby names. It won't be decided by me, but I might get some say. "Has Preston told his parents yet?"

"No, we aren't really telling anyone yet. It's still early. We just found out. We wanted to wait until I was a lot further along. So, if you could not say anything, please?" She looked pleadingly at me.

"That's going to be hard to keep under my hat. But, you have my word." I crossed my heart with my finger.

As we arrived back to the house, people were sitting around with plates in their laps. Men were sitting on truck beds and on tree stumps. Cindy and I made our way into the house to get something to eat. It was hard, having a secret. I so wanted to shout it to the sky. It was especially hard as I passed

Betsy to not grab her and say, *Guess what!*

After everyone was done eating, the ladies put leftovers into containers and stored them in the refrigerator to be carried home later. Emptied dishes were washed and the owners collected them to take to their vehicles. Trash was bagged and put in pick-up beds to be hauled to the dump the next day. Everyone joined in with the others outside. A small bond fire had been lit. The children, with adult supervision, were roasting marshmallows. The musicians had started up again. With the last of the sugar cane ground, the stirrers were hard at work, keeping the molasses from sticking and scorching at the bottom of the cooking troughs. We could all smell its sweetness.

Conversations ranged from the men talking about weather to bragging about crops and the women talking about their families. This one's getting married. That one is having yet another child. This one is moving away, that one is coming back. The older women talked about their health. The younger women talked about who was going with who.

The teenagers were talking about school, horses, and their 4-H projects.

The little ones, tummies full, were beginning to yawn and get cranky.

As the night was winding down, clean quart canning jars were produced.

As jar by jar was filled with the sweet brown liquid, the crowd was disbursing and saying their thanks and goodbyes, each one grateful for the experience. With waves, one by one made their way to their cars and trucks.

I was taking more than a jar of molasses home. I had a special secret in my pocket as well. As Cindy and Preston were climbing in their truck to head back to the city, I caught up with them and gave them a great big hug, and they both hugged back. "Call if you need anything," I said into Cindy's hair as she embraced me tightly.

For the first time in our relationship, I was the first to let go.

Lots of people use the term "best day ever." This one was right up there for me.

Chapter 33

We got an anonymous call. Rather, Aunt Millie answered the phone about horses that were spotted, malnourished and abandoned on a farm two counties away.

I called the local veterinarian's office to arrange for a vet to go with us and look the animals over. Our usual vet, Dr. Conway, who was approaching retirement, was unavailable. His replacement would be accompanying us.

Ranger loaded up the horse trailer, and we headed down the road. It rattled and creaked behind us, making more noise than usual because it was empty. It was much smoother going when we reached the state highway.

It being a Sunday, the vet clinic wasn't busy at all. I waited in the truck while Ranger went in. He came back out with a tall, slim fellow wearing a Stetson. After a few minutes of conversation, they parted ways. Ranger climbing into his truck reported, "He knows where it is. He's going to lead the way."

We followed along the highway for about an hour. Pulling off onto what wasn't much more than a dirt road, we traveled for about twenty more minutes before stopping on the roadside. In the middle of an overgrown briar field sat a dilapidated barn. Leaning drastically, it looked like a gust of wind could blow it over.

"You get the trailer ready." Ranger gave me a level look. "And keep your head on a swivel. This is strictly a stealth operation."

Trusting him, I nodded, just as if I knew what he was talking about.

Ranger cut the barb wire fence, curled it back to the cedar posts on either side, and began to high step his way into the overgrown field.

As quietly as I could, I opened the trailer doors and slid out the ramp. I could see Ranger's cap and the new vet's hat bobbing through the brush as they approached the barn.

I strained my ears to hear any commotion. All I could hear was the call of a circling hawk with an occasional puff of wind. After what seemed like an eternity passing, I spotted the ears of two horses very slowly making their way toward me.

As they got closer, I could see Ranger crouched down leading one, and our helper leading the other. Without a word, they pulled the animals, who looked half-starved and were covered in sores, into the trailer. "Let's roll," said our new friend.

Closing up the trailer, we followed the vet's truck quickly down the road. We made about a quarter of a mile before hearing a shot gun blast, followed by a second one. Ranger sped up, bouncing us over the rutted road. When we reached the highway, he pulled over into a service station.

Without a word, the vet hopped from his truck and climbed into the horse trailer with a medical bag. After administering attention to the horses for some time, he came back out, filled two feed bags and water buckets from his truck and returned to the trailer.

"Are we horse thieves?" I asked Ranger, concerned.

Ranger laughed, "No, I don't think so."

Our new stranger, cohort in crime, finished in the trailer and stored all his equipment. Coming back to the truck cab on Ranger's side, he handed Ranger a piece of paper. "Here are owner slips for the horses. I'll be out later to see about how they are settling in." Tipping his hat, he headed back to his truck.

"Okay," I started. "Spill. Who is this guy?" I asked Ranger.

"I'm thinking he was our anonymous caller," Ranger teased.

"How so?"

"Two plus two. He knew where the farm was. He had already figured out how to get in and out without detection. I hope we didn't just horse nap these poor unfortunate creatures." He nodded his head toward the horse trailer.

"No." I doubted it. "Doc Conway wouldn't have hired him if he was a criminal."

Ranger pointed the truck toward home. I routinely checked the side mirror, on alert, in case we were followed.

Commodore was stomping excitedly from the adjoining field. He watched, neighing a greeting as we unloaded the abused horses into the corral.

You could see their skeletal frame perfectly. My chest ached watching them, heads slumped, ears lowered, accepting the defeat of life. Both were mares, one black and the other a paint. Weeping sores lay open across their legs and back. I didn't even want to think about what story their teeth would tell.

"Lord, have mercy." Ranger wiped his face on his sleeve.

At that time, we heard a motor coming down the road. It was our possible mystery caller, the undercover vet. With long easy steps, he was inside the corral. Hand outreached, he shook with Ranger. Tipping his hat, he said, "I don't believe I've had the pleasure." He gazed down on me.

I was met with eyes of green, or aqua blue. Finding my voice, I extended my hand. "Ann Cantrell, Millie Carson's niece."

His shake was firm but gentle. "Cameron Matheson. Please, call me Cam." His voice was deep and smooth. I found that I couldn't take my eyes off him with his square jaw and a slight cleft in his chin. My brain was thinking, *Dudley Do Right lives.*

"I suppose I owe you all an explanation," he began.

He had our full attention. "Yes, that would be nice," Ranger acknowledged.

"The man that had these horses was at one time a trainer and the go-to man for breaking a wild horse." He paused. "He has seen better days. We filed the proper paperwork. We attempted a rescue a week ago with no success. He came out, rifle in hand, and wasn't having it.

He needs help but won't accept it. He's a widower with dementia and no family to aid the situation. I couldn't just walk away and let these girls die."

He removed his hat and shook his head. "I heard of the work you did here and was relieved to have somewhere to bring them. You're not going to be in any trouble. As you can see from their condition, he may have forgotten he still had these two; that is, until we showed up to rescue them. Thank goodness, he wasn't a very good shot. I'm sorry to have put you in danger. I didn't expect him to be out in the field. I'll cover whatever the cost there may be for their keep, medication, and food. I hope you understand. I couldn't just walk away. You can still say no, and I'll make other arrangements."

"I would have done the same," I hear myself saying. "Do you think they have a chance?" Looking at the condition of them, I wonder.

"I pray they do," he said earnestly.

"Well, Dr. Matheson. Looks like we'll be seeing a lot of you." I blushed. Really, Ann?

"Please, just Cam. I suppose you will." He grinned back at me.

"Excuse me," Ranger grunted. "Best get the trailer and truck stowed away. Pleased to meet you." He laughed as he strolled away.

When Ranger was no longer in earshot, Cam leaned toward me. "I apologize for asking, but are you single, Ann? May I call you Ann?"

I loved hearing him say my name. It was soft and silky. "Why yes, yes I am, and yes you may," I stammered. I'm such a nerd.

"Excellent," he answered with a huge smile. "Let's get these special girls squared away."

"I'd be honored to help." I smiled back.

We spent the next several hours making the black horse we dubbed Mary and the paint we named Martha comfortable. Leading Commodore back to his stall, he stomped his impatience, eager to meet his new friends. Talking softly to him, I explained that the girls were hurt and needed to heal. He seemed to understand after looking in on them in their stalls. I gave him an extra-long brushing before leaving him for the night.

Aunt Millie was making her appointed nightly visit. Cam and I met her midway into her walk. I introduced him, holding my breath. Her opinion means everything.

Cam was pleasant and at ease with her, his respect shining through.

As she turned to make her visit, she gave me a wink.

My face must show my every emotion.

Leaning against his truck, Cam looked at me with a tilt to his head. "I'll be back tomorrow with a Ferrier to tend to their hooves. They may also need some work on their teeth. It's hard for them to eat with bad teeth."

"See you tomorrow then," I said, balancing on one foot with my hands behind my back.

I'm acting like a lovesick schoolgirl. Gathering what was left of my pride, I gave a little wave and marched myself into the house.

Pulling the door open, I almost ran into Betsy. "Give!" she insisted. "Who's Mr. Cutie Pie?"

"The new vet that's seeing to the rescued horses," I answered nonchalantly. "Dr. Cameron Matheson."

"Uh-huh." She wasn't buying it. "Ann's got a boyfriend." She began to sing a song over and over.

"Oh, stop." I scolded her as I turned to peer out the window, watching him leave. "He'll be back tomorrow. I wonder what's wrong with him. I mean, how can you be all that and a bag of chips and not have a flaw or two?"

"Don't borrow trouble, Ann, as my old mother used to say." Betsy shook her head at me.

I nodded my head in agreement and went to the mud room to remove my boots and wash the day's activities off my hands.

Brian came bounding in with Bill in his wake. "Hey, met the new vet on the road. He seems like a great guy. Told me all about the new horses. Asked me about a million questions about you, Mom. I think he's, as the country folks say, sweet on you." He poked me with his elbow and snickered.

Bill nudged me for his treat. I pulled a raw hide from the bag in the cabinet. "Sit!" I commanded. After a little rub under the chin, I gave him the chewy treat. It was a relief to busy myself and hide my reddening face.

Betsy overheard Brian and started up teasing again. Brian grabbed an apple and winked at me before he and his dog jetted back outside.

I scurried upstairs to the sanctity of my room. Plopping down at my dresser, I rested my hot face in my hands and stared in the mirror. What could that kind of man possibly see in me?

Whatever it was, it wasn't written on my rosy cheeks. For some reason, I felt like spiking a ball and doing a victory dance. Instead, I lay on my bed and stared at the ceiling. What if he sees the farm and is thinking, money or land? There I go borrowing trouble. Still, I must proceed with caution. I'm about to be a grandmother. I've got to keep my head.

As it started getting dark, I made my way to the barn to check on our new occupants. The black, Mary, was nickering and somewhat agitated. Martha was standing so still. It looked like every movement was painful to her. "It's going to be okay. I know you've had a rough go of things. But you're in a good place now with people that will care for you. So, you can relax and heal. There're lots of good things that will happen for you very soon. Believe me, I should know. I wasn't as battered as you, but look at me now."

"You give awfully good advice," Aunt Millie whispered from behind me. "I'm so glad you are all here. There's so much life in the place now. I wish I had brought you on sooner."

Bending to Martha, she stroked her nose with her arthritic hand. "Mm, mm, mm," she murmured. "You poor girls."

Commodore stomped and snorted his jealousy. Aunt Millie laughed. "You'll get your turn, ole boy."

"So, what do you know about the new vet?" I pressed.

"Dr. Conway has a good opinion of him. But I'm not telling you a thing, and I'll tell you why." She adjusted her position with her walking stick. "Half the fun is getting to know someone." She grinned.

"Well. I just might do that," I giggled.

Here I am, mid-forties, feeling like a kid again.

Chapter 34

The new day found Mary to be more energized and curious about her surroundings. Martha, however, was still lethargic and had developed a wheeze. In the cold morning air, you could see puffs of misty clouds pouring from her labored breath. She must be in a lot of pain.

Gathering plastic sheeting from the green house, I made her stall as airtight as possible and covered her with a horse blanket to hold in her body heat. This seems sensible but I hope it's the right thing to do. After mucking her stall, laying down fresh hay, and seeing to her water and food, I left her with a promise to do all I could to make her well.

I met with Ranger and completed a few chores before I looked in on her again. She had eaten some of her oats but continued to make a whistling noise with every intake of air. By sunup, the day had warmed enough to remove her covering. Avoiding her sores, I gave her a rub down. She responded with affection to my touch.

Looking in on Mary, I found her restless. I let her out of her stall and walked her slowly to the corral. She stood in the sunlight, shaking her coat, enjoying the fresh air. Commodore noticed us and came running from the field enclosure. I introduced them. Mary backed up a little and then ignored him while he pranced around. I rubbed her neck. "Aren't boys silly?" I cooed to her.

My cell phone jingled. Pulling it from my back pocket, I could see that it was the veterinarian's office. "Hello," I answered.

"Good morning, Ann. This is Cam. How are the girls today?"

Moving away from Mary, I leaned against the side of the barn. "Mary seems more robust, but Martha has a rasp. I'm not sure what to do for her."

"Just keep her quiet and in her stall. I'm just about done here, then I'll be heading your way with a Ferrier to look at their hooves. That be okay for you all?" he asked.

"Yep," I answered.

"See you then," he said slowly as if he were distracted. I could hear barking in the background before he ended the call.

What's your story? I wondered. Last thing I need is another toxic relationship consuming my life. What am I doing? I need to get my head on straight. There is so much to be done before winter.

With Preston gone, the rest of us have extra duty. Fortunately, Gil has come to help. We are pushed to complete the end of season jobs and attend to the greenhouses, which will provide income for us to get through the next season. There is a lot of pressure, keeping things going.

Closing the corral gate, I started to the greenhouses to help them with prepping the beds for the next round of planting. A section was set up for broccoli, greens, cauliflower, cabbages, and radishes. After several hours of digging out dead roots and refilling containers with compost and soil, I was a mess.

When the others left for lunch break, I waved them off. This needed to be completed before the end of the day.

The other greenhouse would have flowers and wreaths for the holidays. Setting up a craft area for creating holiday items to sell at the farmers market is exciting. This needs to be completed before Cindy and Preston finish their fall semester.

I'm not entirely on board with their big plans. If they turned the house into a Bed and Breakfast, where would we all live? I think it would be a better idea to convert one of the barns into the B & B and use the house for meals. Maybe I'll pitch my idea to Cindy and see how it flies. She may be underestimating how time-consuming caring for a child can be.

I vaguely remember the youthful excitement of being so full of ideas and possibilities. It's good to see Cindy coming into her own, becoming independent and fearless of hard work.

We hadn't heard a peep from Jake since the wedding. I wonder what he's been up to these past months. Probably found himself someone to take care of his needs by now. I hope he has. Even with the way things went for us, I don't wish him to be alone. Maybe I should wish the same thing for myself.

The men returned from their lunch break, laughing about something Brian had said.

"He's telling jokes," Ranger answered my questioning look.

"What did one eye say to the other eye?" Brian grinned.

"I don't know." I played along.

"Something between us smells." He laughed for effect.

Ranger and Gil shook their heads.

"That's terrible," I responded, my stomach growing.

Brian thought of another joke. "When is your stomach like an angry animal? When it growls!" He poked my abdomen with his finger.

Ranger put on his work gloves. "Alright. Let's get back at it. Looks like we just might get this done today. It's supposed to rain by the end of the week. We've got hay to bale before that happens. While it's raining, we will get on the other greenhouse."

"Sounds like a plan," I answer. "Think I'll head to the house and get a bite to eat, settle down the angry animal in my stomach." I winked at Brian.

"Cam is at the barn seeing to the horses," Ranger said, not looking at me.

"Yeah, okay." I shrug, keeping it nonchalant. "I look a mess, but I'm sure he's seen worse."

"Well, good on you. Give him warts and all." Brian slapped me on the back, dust rising in the air. Brian and Gil laughed. Ranger looked on with an expression I had never seen before. Was it protectiveness, jealousy, or my imagination?

I opened the door of the greenhouse and peered out. The coast looked clear. Come on coward, just go about your business. I made it as far as Aunt Millie's azalea bushes before I spotted them in the corral with both the mares. The Ferrier was set up, working on Martha's hooves. Cam spotted me and waved. I waved back, a little too enthusiastically, before I could stop myself. I think I'm in trouble. Lord, Lord. Let him be one of the good guys.

The Ferrier spoke, distracting Cam. I ducked into the mudroom and began to peel off my sodden outer clothing and muddy boots. Washing my hands and arms at the sink, I removed as much as I could with Aunt Millie's soap and scrub brush.

Scurrying into the kitchen, I find that Betsy and Aunt Millie had left me a note on the fridge. "Gone to town for hair appointments, your lunch is in the oven." I checked the floor to see if my socks were leaving a trail. I was good. Hopping up the stairs, I took a quick shower. Dressing in clean jeans and a sweatshirt, I raked a comb through my wet hair and headed downstairs to eat.

Grabbing a potholder from the drawer, I pulled a plate of stew and corn bread from the oven and cut off the heat. With a glass of milk, I made my way to the office to check emails and phone messages while I nibbled.

After finishing, I washed my plate, spoon and glass and placed them in the drainer. All the while, with every movement, I felt the pull of Cam being there, near. I should probably go back to the greenhouse and help the guys some more. Before I could have another thought, my phone rang. It was Cindy.

"Hey sweetheart," I answered.

"Hey, Mom. I have a favor to ask." She sounded anxious.

"Sure, anything. What do you need?" My mom intuition was revving up. Something's wrong. Is it the baby?

"Preston and I just had the most horrible argument. He stormed out and I don't know where he's gone. I want to come home." She cried little burp like sobs.

"Oh, honey. Couples fight. I'm sure he'll be back. Just give him a little time to cool down and before you know it, in he will walk, and you will work it out." I tried to sound optimistic.

"But Mom, we both said some awful things. I don't think he will ever be able to forgive me. I called him a neat freak and well, as you know, clutter doesn't bother me that much. He thinks I will be a horrible mom because I can't ever find the car keys," she blubbered.

I tried hard to not respond with a laugh. She was so upset. But I could see where this was going. Time for some tough love.

"Cynthia, I really can't help you. You're a married woman now and you need to settle this yourself. It's between you and your husband. Work it out."

"Hah!" she shouted. "Way to defend your daughter, Mom," she said sarcastically. "How dare you take his side. I'm pregnant," She wailed.

"Not taking sides, staying out of your marriage," I responded evenly. "When he comes back, try to meet him halfway. Talk it out. Make it right," I advised. "I love you, my daughter. But I want you to woman up. Be a wife to him. Be on his team."

There was silence on the other end of the phone. I heard her blowing her nose. "I guess I could clean the place up some. That would show him that I hear him."

"That's the spirit. You and Preston are to be in each other's corner. That's how it's supposed to work," I stated.

"Thanks, Mom, I gotta go."

"I love you," I said. But, I think she had already disconnected.

Putting my cell in my back pocket, I made my way outside. Deciding to take my own advice of bravery, I march to the corral. Ranger, Brian, and Gil had come out of the greenhouse and were with Cam, fussing over the mares who were enjoying the attention.

I put my hair up into a ponytail with an elastic band and put a smile on my face. Bill came over for a nuzzle and to trot beside me, giving me an escort. I'm so happy to be a part of this team.

Climbing over the fence, I asked Cam, "How are they looking?" He was squatted down, applying salve to Martha's legs.

"Much better." He smiled up at me, making my heart skip a beat. "I can bunk here tonight, just to keep a close eye on the paint, Martha?" he asked.

I nodded yes.

"She's doing well except for one of the wounds along her flank," he said with relief. "I'm going to give her antibiotics as well. I may need to drain fluid off her lungs if this wheezing continues." He stood, rubbing Martha's mane.

"We got a good look at their teeth; fortunately, only Mary, the black, needs some attention to a couple of hers. The Ferrier's been working on their hooves and should have them completely shoed in a couple of hours. I'd like to make some changes to their stalls, if I may. Fresh hay and such." He was businesslike.

"Sure, whatever you need." I looked to Ranger, he nodded agreement.

Cam was so serious, he had me worried. I've never dealt with an ill horse before. I'm glad he is here.

Chapter 35

I tossed and turned all night. Every time I closed my eyes, I would get the horses, Cindy, or Cam on my mind. I finally gave up at four and got dressed.

Following the glow of Aunt Millie's lights, I made my way to the barn. I heard Cam talking to Martha. "It's okay, girl. You're going to be just fine."

"Hi," I greeted them at the stall door. "Rough night?"

"Hi." He turned, looking red-eyed and tired. "I did end up draining her. She began improving right away. I think she will be in the pink again soon. Come in. Listen to her breathing."

I moved inside. Cam got on one knee. Putting his stethoscope to her chest, he handed me the other end to put in my ears. Sure enough, her breathing wasn't labored anymore.

"That's a relief," I sighed.

"Ann?" he asked. "I," he swallowed, looking up at me. "I'd like to get to know you. I know we are practically strangers. Do you think you might be interested in an odd fellow like me?"

"Why me?" I took a step back. "Why are you interested in me? Is there something wrong with you?" I asked softly.

"Depends on who you ask," he responded, standing. "I guess I should tell you my story." He stood, clearing his throat. "I was married," he paused. "My wife, Carrie, couldn't have children. I thought we would be okay. I came to terms with it, but the more time passed, the worse her jealousy got. She needed constant assurance. If I paid any attention to anyone or anything else, it set her off. She was jealous of our pets, our neighbors, my coworkers. It got so bad, we went for counseling. Adoption was not an option for her. If she couldn't have her own child, she didn't want one that came from someone else." He stood straighter.

"Eventually, she gave up on our marriage and divorced me. It's like, she wasn't complete if she couldn't have children and wanted me to be as miserable as she was. She's living near her family in Texas now. We've had no contact. It's strange to have a marriage one day and nothing the next. She took our dogs with her, too. It's been close to five years now." He looked sad, staring at the hay on the floor. "I might miss the dogs even more than what we had."

"What about your family?" I asked, thinking how blessed I am to have mine.

"I was in foster care most of my life, never knew my father. They told me that my mother was a drug addict. She gave me up before I was school age." He looked hurt with a hint of embarrassment.

His expression made my heart ache. He became silent. I felt it was my turn.

"My story?" I asked, putting my hand to my chest.

He nodded and I continued. "I'm not close with my parents either. My dad is a minister, and my mother is a minister's wife. I've been nothing but a disappointment to her, and he goes whatever direction she deems right."

I touched his arm, lightly. "But my Aunt Millie loves me. She always has. Since I was a little girl, I could feel her love for me. I'm sorry you haven't known that."

"She's a special lady, like you." Moisture glistened in his eyes.

Patting his arm, I changed the subject. "What made you decide to become a vet?"

"Love of animals, unconditional love." He looked at me tenderly. "When I look at you, I can see your capacity to love. It glows out of you like a shinning beacon from a lighthouse."

Martha neighed loudly, causing us both to laugh.

I whispered to him, "I've been through some hard things for the last few years. I don't know if I trust myself to begin something."

Stepping away from him, I wait for a response.

"I just want to be around you. You get there when you get there." He shrugged his shoulders.

"What if I'm never ready?" I held still.

Standing up to his full height, he opened his arms wide. "May I hold you for just a moment?" His eyes pleaded.

Stepping slowly into his embrace, I rested my head in the crook of his neck and held my breath while he enveloped me with his strong arms. Slowly exhaling, I felt safe, secure, and comfortable. My heart lurched in my chest, I could hear it beating in my ears.

Simultaneously, we leaned backward, facing each other. "Ann?" Cam asked lowly. I could see the fine stubble of new salt and pepper growth on his handsome chin. Then, making my way up to look into his eyes, I knew I was in trouble for sure.

"Yes, Cam?" I checked out.

"May I court you?" He smiled and laughed lowly.

"Maybe." I smiled back.

We heard voices coming into the barn. It would probably be Ranger, preparing the equipment for the day.

Stepping awkwardly away from each other, I blinked to stop my spinning head. Looking over at Cam, I can see he is having a similar reaction. Hooking his thumbs into his belt loops, he was grinning, shaking his head.

Heat rose to my cheeks. I put my hands to my face to cool down.

Bill appeared at the top of the stall door. Yelping his good morning greeting, he scratched to be let in. Cracking the door, I blocked his entry. "Good morning, boy." I patted his soft, furry head. I looked back at Cam before walking away. He was standing the same with that big smile still in place.

Courting? Really, Ann? Oh my.

Ranger was just hooking the spreader on the back of the tractor as I came around the corner. "Mornin'. You're up early, Ann."

"Had a little trouble sleeping. So, I guess it's hay day. Could you use some help?" I asked a little too brightly.

Brian came out of the bunkhouse and whistled for Bill. He took off toward his master in a run.

"Yep, got several neighbors coming to help get the hay in. You could drive the truck for us." He nodded.

"Let me get a hat and tell them in the house and we'll get her done." My heart was singing with every step. Feeling this happy is foreign to me, but I sure could get used to it.

Chapter 36

We've had our first frost. Fortunately, most of our harvest is completed. After storing what hay we needed, the surplus was so great, we were able to sell some and donate the rest to our helpful neighbors.

Cindy and Preston came home for fall break. They made their announcement to the family about the pregnancy. I was glad to no longer be holding that secret. Betsy was a little upset with me for not telling her. She couldn't hold a grudge for long with everyone so thrilled. Brian was especially happy when he found out that it was going to be a boy. Preston wanted to name the baby after his dad, Mike, his given name of Michael.

When I questioned Cindy about Jake, if he knew, she just shrugged. Her face fell as she gently rubbed her swelling belly. Apparently, they weren't having much contact.

"He is only interested if I make the effort and go to him. He doesn't want to come visit. Says it's because Betsy's condo is across from where you were living when you betrayed him by leaving us. He also says that he is extremely busy," she said using finger quotes in the air.

I could tell she was upset by her father's rejection, but he did deserve to know he is going to be a grandfather. It's not my place to say anything, thank goodness.

After the seasonal transition, my days were once again becoming routine. The only exception is I have begun to spend some of the day shadowing

Aunt Millie. With her health improving, I want to take advantage of her wisdom and learn all that I can of her way of doing things.

Many of our conversations end with what she would like to see happen after she is gone. I sometimes change the subject. But, lately, I try hard to remember everything she suggests. I have taken to writing them down at night in a journal.

Any spare time I have, I spend working in the greenhouse. We set up a drying station for the plants that are to be used in the crafts. I am enjoying exercising my creative muscles. The decorated wreaths are starting to pile up. Brian came up with a great idea of rigging up a support system from the ceiling. It got them out of the way, yet kept them safe from any destruction until they could be transported for selling at the market. Bird houses and displays with little red trucks were popular too. Betsy had an undiscovered talent for painting. She created country winter scenes with old barn wood. Red cardinals and snow-covered fences were her favorite to paint. She always brought music to the greenhouse. Listening to carols helped put us all in a holiday mood. Aunt Millie, feeling left out, had me bring in her rocker from the porch. She would rock in time to the merriment.

Lately, when I have my evening meeting with Ranger, he has begun to speak of his departure for Alaska. It makes me sad to listen to his plans for retirement. I will be glad to have Cindy and Preston return, but I know it will mean that Ranger is getting closer to his exit. I've become accustomed to change and starting over, but I will miss his strong presence. Having him here makes me feel safe and secure in keeping the farm healthy and productive.

Several times, I have found him staring at me, as if he wanted to say or ask me something. When I ask, "What is it?" he just shakes his head and goes back to whatever task we are doing. I wish he would just say what's on his mind. Could be that he is wondering if we are all going to be able to manage without him. I know I'm wondering that myself. Just the same, it sure would be nice to know what his thoughts are.

With Cam's help, the horses are all in great health. He is becoming an everyday part of the farm. Most nights, he has supper with us. It's somewhat of a drive from town where he lives at the veterinarian office in the modest, efficiency apartment. He says it's all he needs considering what little time he is there.

Our dating isn't quite like a whirlwind romance. It's more of a slow building of a special relationship. Cam jumps in to help out with whatever is going on at the farm. It's great having a help mate when you're mucking out the horses' stalls or moving cattle. He has an instinct of knowing what needs to be done and how it's accomplished.

Working side by side, we are getting to know each other quite well. We have deep conversations on long sunset walks. Sometimes we just sit, arms wrapped around each other, watching the sun go behind the ridge.

The days are getting shorter and shorter. The holidays are coming fast. My cousin, Aaron, will be coming for Thanksgiving with his family, and hopefully Emily too. The last time we were all together, I still had awkward teenage acne. I'm excited to see them again and have all of the family under one roof.

Aunt Millie wants to invite my parents as well. I can't refuse her request, no matter how uncomfortable their presence is for me. I'm hoping that they will look around the farm at all we have accomplished and realize that what we are doing here is not only acceptable but invaluable. That could happen, right?

Poor Betsy has been making menus, gathering food, asking about allergies and food preferences for weeks. Just when she thinks she has a complete head count of attendees, someone remembers another person that they have invited. At last count, it's between seventeen and twenty people. I assured her that everyone will pitch in to prepare the house and the meal.

Before heading back to take finals and complete their semester, Cindy and Preston asked it would be okay for his parents could join us for Thanksgiving. Betsy began to fan her face with her apron.

"Sure," she answered with an eye roll.

Preston noticed and apologized. "I'm sorry. Maybe I should have let you know sooner?"

"No, honey." Betsy immediately regretted her reaction. "I'm the one that's sorry. I tell you what. I'm going to round up to thirty." She smiled and patted his arm.

I don't think he understood what she meant by that. But he was too polite to question her.

Cindy, upon exiting at the door, popped her head back in. "I've invited Dad, and he is bringing a guest." She then made her getaway as Betsy threw her apron at the closing door.

"Have mercy!" Betsy cried out.

I couldn't help myself. I laughed at her. As realization of what Cindy said hit me, I stopped laughing. Cam and Jake would be in the same room. Uh-oh.

Betsy and I both looked at each other like deer in the headlights.

"Well, gobble, gobble," I said sarcastically.

Chapter 37

Happy Thanksgiving!

Everyone in the house was up early. The morning chores were completed by the time the sun had topped the ridge. The animals seemed to sense that it was a special day as we all hurried through our routines. Life on the farm doesn't stop, even for holidays.

Last night's preparations left us with only last-minute dishes to prepare for our noon meal.

Furniture was rearranged in the living area for a make-shift table to accommodate everyone. Aunt Millie's largest bowls and platters were brought from the back of cabinets. Several gallons of sweet tea had been brewed. The sideboard was covered with pumpkin and pecan pies along with Aunt Millie's stack cake and a carrot cake with cream cheese frosting. Every time I passed by the latter, my mouth watered.

Two twenty-pound turkeys were roasting in the oven. The dressing was made and cranberry sauce was chilling in the refrigerator. Aunt Millie was working on deviled eggs while Betsy chopped cabbage for coleslaw. I was on potato duty, peeling as efficiently as I could. Betsy had brought several quarts of the green beans from the cellar that she had canned in the summer.

Cindy and Preston had stayed overnight. Aunt Millie's children, Aaron and Emily, had canceled at the last minute. Aaron's family were staying home in Virginia. Their two children had the flu and couldn't travel. Emily was having her time off with friends. This made me sad for Aunt Millie; her children were not coming to see her. I'm glad that she has the rest of us here with her. She did talk on the phone for a long time with each of them. I suppose that's better than nothing. Still, it's not the same as spending time together.

Cindy was laying out place settings on the tables. Every few minutes, she would pause and stretch her back. She was carrying her baby boy low, causing her discomfort.

Ranger, Brian, and Gil had put out extra seating on the front porch. The white tablecloths were billowing in the breeze. We were so fortunate to have a mild, sunny day, making outdoor eating possible.

The fellows were all glad to have Preston back. We could hear them giving him a hard time, teasing him about being an old married man. He was dishing it right back at them. "You all are just jealous. Just wait until you see my kid. You'll turn green with envy."

With the food prep well underway, we all decided to make ourselves presentable for company. I had bought a new dress and was looking forward to showing it off to Cam. With the exception of church on Sundays, I didn't have many opportunities to dress up for him.

It didn't seem to matter to him. Whether I was smelling of soap and perfume or covered in mud, he treated me with the same affection and attention. I'm so happy, I'm sure that I'm obnoxious, always humming or dancing around. I just can't seem to help myself.

Preston's parents were the first to arrive. Melissa greeted me with a warm embrace. Mike shook hands with just about everyone. They had brought a beautiful bouquet of flowers with them.

Handing the flowers to Betsy, Melissa said, "My mother always told me, it's impolite to go to someone's home empty-handed."

"Thank you, they are beautiful," Betsy exclaimed. Taking the bouquet, she disappeared into the pantry to get a vase.

Melissa's eyes danced as she talked with Cindy about the grandchild she couldn't wait to meet. Cindy made my heart swell with her peaceful, loving expression as Melissa placed her hands to feel the baby kick. This child is going to be so spoiled.

Melissa asked for an apron. She wanted to help in the kitchen. "After all, we are family." She smiled. Betsy was happy to comply.

With all of us pitching in, we had all the platters of food completed in short work.

My parents arrived next. Entering the house, they were stiffly polite. They both looked thin and withered to me. When had they aged so much?

Aunt Millie pulled my dad away, escorting him into the office. My mother's worried eye movements were a sign of her discomfort. She must be dying to know what her sister-in-law is saying to her husband.

My cell phone vibrated; it was Cam.

"Hi, dinner's ready and people are arriving. Are you on your way?"

"I'm going to be a little late, if I can make it at all. I'm sorry. We have an injured dog, and I just can't leave him. It's touch and go. I'm so, so sorry, Ann. I was so looking forward to that turkey, and you, of course." He chuckled.

"I understand. It can't be helped," I said, trying to sound earnest but not feeling it. "I'll make you up a plate and bring it to you later if you can't come. How's that?"

"You're a peach! That would be awesome, thanks," he said.

"Okay, hope the doggie makes it."

"Again, Ann, I'm sorry," he said sincerely. "Catch you later."

Disconnecting, I felt disappointment but some relief to not have him meeting my parents yet or Jake. "Cam had an emergency so he's not coming," I informed Betsy. "I'll make him up a plate, maybe take it to him afterwards."

"That's a good idea." She patted my arm. "Why don't you go ahead and prepare it, just in case. It could be lean pickings later on." She untied the stings on her apron and hung it on the hook.

I had just slid Cameron's covered plate into the refrigerator when I heard Brian call out, "Dad's here. What the? You've got to be kidding me!"

"What is it?" I asked, hurrying to his side.

"He has Shirley with him," Brian said angrily.

"Perfect," I said a little too loudly. "I guess your dad is her fallback guy.

The other one must have not worked out." My parents are going to flip out.

Looking around, I didn't see my mother. I was more worried about her reaction than anyone else's.

Betsy leaped to my side as Shirley came breezing into the room, carrying a bowl of banana pudding. "Ann, before you say anything, I must apologize to you. I was just awful to you and your family. I pray you can let bygones be bygones," she pleaded.

I looked at Betsy; she looked at me. We both looked at Shirley, all dolled up in chiffon and heavy makeup. "Sure, Shirley," I answered. Well, what else could I say? She's pitiful.

Cindy and my mother came down the stairs, stopping on the bottom step.

"Dad, you came!" Cindy ran to hug him. Then, spying Shirley, she stepped back. "What's she doing here? Oh, Dad, don't tell me you're back with her?" Her face fell.

"Yes, sweetheart. I am. She's good for me." He looked sincere, bless his sorry heart.

I couldn't stop the thought, but not your wallet.

Cindy looked to me for confirmation. I shrugged and smiled at her. *Let's not upset the pregnant lady, people.*

"We're getting married at Christmas, and I'd like you and Brian to be there," Jake went on.

The room went silent. Cindy shot daggers from her eyes to Shirley. My mother put her hand to her mouth and swooned. Brian was the first to get to her, just catching her before she collapsed.

"Happy Thanksgiving, everybody!" I called out just as Aunt Millie and my dad came out of the office.

All heads turned to them. They were both rubbing their eyes with hankies and sniffling. Reading the room, they looked at each other, then at me.

"Don't even ask," I stated flatly. Judging by their emotion, Aunt Millie must have told my dad about her health status.

Noticing my mother, my father leapt to her side, relieving Brian.

Suddenly, Bond Winston and Ranger came in the front door. In all the excitement I hadn't heard any cars pull up.

"I could practically smell that turkey down the road," smiled Bond. "Happy Thanksgiving, everyone. I don't believe we've met." He made a beeline for Shirley.

"Bond, Shirley," I introduced them. It figures—two of a kind would gravitate toward each other. "My ex-husband's fiancée."

That seemed to please Shirley but not Bond. He stepped back like he had gotten too close to a hot stove.

With Brian's help, my father settled his wife into the nearest chair with a glass of water and comforted her. Watching their movements gave me déjà vu; somehow I would be blamed for all of this.

Aunt Millie broke the ice with her frail voice. "Brother, would you please say a prayer to bless our meal?" She nodded toward my dad. "And you might ought to make it a really good one." She pursed her lips.

The men removed their hats. We all bowed our heads.

"Lord, we come to you today grateful for the blessings of life. Thankful for the family and friends you've seen fit to be here together and those that could not be with us today. You know the concerns and needs of each heart, the plans you have for each and every one of us. Be with us today. Give us your peace and holy understanding. Bless this food to the nourishment of our bodies and fit us for heaven to meet with you there." His strong baritone voice cracked on the last word. Aunt Millie reached over and touched his hand. And everyone said, "Amen."

"Just think, this time next year, there will be a little one at the table," I said to cheer everyone. "Let's all grab a plate and get our grub on."

My mother, somewhat recovered, shook her head at me. Making her way to my side, she asked, "So, this is your life now?" She tipped her head to indicate all my mistakes.

"Yep, ain't it great?" I nudged her with my elbow.

"Well, I never!" she exclaimed.

"Loosen up, Mother Dearest," I teased her.

Lowering my voice, I whispered to her, "You're missing so much by holding such a standard. Look around at these people. All I see are humans just trying to make a connection. All you seem to see are errors and inadequacies. If you can let go of your judgments, you will be so much happier.

And so will the people around you."

She cocked her quaffed head to look at me from under her eyelids. "I don't judge. God judges. Some of these folks would do well to acknowledge that fact."

"Daniel," she called to my dad.

He ran to her side. She walked him down the hallway, talking closely as he nodded his head.

Mike and Melissa had remained silent though all the much ado. They were now seated with Preston and Cindy, enjoying their food. I think I'd like to sit at that table.

Grabbing a plate, I followed in line with Betsy and Aunt Millie. Bond fell into line behind me, followed by Ranger, Brian, and Gil.

Small talk ensued as we were eating. My parents made their way back into the room and fixed their plates. They took seats next to Betsy and Aunt Millie in the kitchen.

Preston and Cindy answered all the usual questions about the baby. When asked about the name, Mike was pleasantly surprised to have his grandson named after him. Melissa beamed with pride. "Have you decided on the middle name?" she asked.

"We are still thinking on that one." Cindy smiled.

I was glad that Jake and Shirley had taken one of the tables outside. Ranger, Bond, Brian, and Gil were seated at the other outside table. I was dreading Jake's reaction to the baby's name. We didn't need any more drama today.

After the meal, all the women, with the exception of Shirley and my mother, worked in the kitchen, storing leftovers and washing the dishes. Jake and Shirley along with my parents, made their obligated thanks and exited after dessert. Mike and Preston were laying out in the living room watching football. Brian and Gil headed over to Gil's house for more Thanksgiving feasting with Bill in tow. Ranger saw Bond off, then headed out to check on the stock.

This was my favorite part of Thanksgiving—dishes washed, sitting at the kitchen table, laughing over the day with these wonderful ladies.

"I thought Ruth was going to pop a vein when Shirley came in," laughed Betsy.

"I missed all the fun." Aunt Millie frowned.

"I loved every minute of it," said Melissa. "It's usually just me, Mike, and Preston at our Thanksgivings."

"You've got to move closer. You don't want to miss out on seeing that baby grow up," I told her.

"About that," Melissa cocked her pretty eyebrow. "Come the end of the school year, we are looking at relocating." She took a lady-like sip of her coffee.

"Yay!" I hollered.

"Schools are always looking for teachers. Like you said, Ann, I don't want to miss out on that baby growing up. We talked it over and looked into making the move, although I may be the first black teacher in this county." She looked to Aunt Millie for an answer.

"No. I believe there was a science teacher when my children were in school. Mr. Monroe, I think, was his name. He retired some years back," she answered. "We have several families of color that have recently moved here. Some of the children are mixed like Preston. Could be, someday, we'll all be just one race, the human race." She held her hands as if she were praying.

The front door opened, and Cam came in, greeting us all with, "Happy Thanksgiving, everyone!"

I stood and retrieved his plate from the fridge. "The dog?" I asked.

He shook his head. He looked bone tired.

"Here, have a seat." I sat him down in my vacant chair.

Betsy hopped up and got him coffee.

Aunt Millie excused herself and went to lie down. Melissa and Betsy joined the men in the living room. I heard Betsy call out, "That was pass interference! Throw the flag, ref!"

After heating Cam's food in the microwave, I placed his plate in front of him. Taking the chair next to him, we told each other all about our day. He's so good for me. I hope I'm good for him too.

Chapter 38

The Christmas season is upon us. Our crafts and wreaths have been a big hit at the farmer's market. Ranger has barely kept up with the demand for his Christmas trees. We've had our first snow, putting us all in the Christmas mood.

Betsy has gone over the top with decorating. Anything that is standing still has a red bow or garland wrapped around it. Ranger brought in what he called his best tree, a gift for the family. I could see a little cracking around the edges of his tough exterior. It's his last Christmas with us.

When it came to decorating the tree, we made it an evening of celebration. With carols playing in the background, we sipped hot apple cider, and sang along. Some of us were a little off key (Brian and Cam), but we didn't care.

Then, there was the great debate about putting on the icicles. Betsy wanted to separate and place them one at a time. Cindy, whose protruding tummy kept knocking off ornaments, wanted to group them. I didn't want them at all. What a mess they make! Brian's solution was to stand back and throw them at the tree. It didn't matter; I knew Betsy would come behind us later and fix it properly.

The cheerful decorations were a comfort in the gloomy short days. It was dark by late afternoon and often rainy and cold. I mostly felt sympathy for the animals. I know they are wearing a coat and protected, but still, you can feel the cold and damp into your bones. It was as if we all were hunkered down and waiting for sunshine to return. Aunt Millie mostly stayed wrapped up in sweaters with a portable heater at her feet.

There was a stillness to the land, a hibernation. The only movement was the livestock and the people scurrying about. Even our greenhouses were cleared of most plant life. The new cycle would begin come March.

Betsy, Cindy, and Aunt Millie had taken up crocheting and sewing, making clothes and blankets for the baby. Cindy had placed a crib in the bedroom she and Preston share. She planned to make Brian's room into a nursery when the baby got old enough to sleep on his own.

So far, no more plans for a B & B have been mentioned. With the semester completed, the soon-to-be parents were nesting. During the day, Preston and Ranger were inseparable. When Preston takes over the reins of foreman, great responsibility will be placed on his young but capable shoulders. Coupled with first-time fatherhood, he will need all of us supporting him. I'm so glad his parents will be close by, especially Melissa. I look forward to having our friendship grow.

With Cindy and Preston moving out of Betsy's condo, she has decided to put it on the market. This gives me great relief. At any time, she could have decided the farm life wasn't for her and moved back to the city. She will be accompanying the men to move the last of her furniture in the next few weeks. It may be hard for her considering that it will be the last of her life with Carl. She confided in me that all she cares to keep are her photo albums and a couple of Carl's shirts. She plans to make them into pillows for her bed.

Ranger has set his retirement date. As soon as the spring planting is completed, he is setting his hat for Alaska. He has been making calls to relatives and borrowing my computer to look at real estate. I give him privacy when he is in the office, hunting and pecking on the keyboard. His hope is to get a cabin with some acreage. He has extended an open invitation to us all. He said with some difficulty, "I consider you to be part of my family, too."

I have secretly wondered if he's having second thoughts. If that's the case, he could retire right here, live out his days as a consultant to Preston.

I'm going to tuck that idea away for now and bring it back out if the opportunity presents itself.

Cam has been more absent lately. I mostly see him on weekends. With the days being so much shorter, there is less time to spend outside. I'm hoping that's the reason for his staying in town at the vet clinic more. He acts the same, even misses me when we aren't together. I need to prepare myself for the heartbreak just in case he has lost interest.

On the downside, if he calls us off, it will hurt a lot for a long time. I need to be okay, either way. I don't want my life tangled up in a man again. His presence, his behavior, can't determine how I feel about myself or my life.

He does call every night at bedtime to go over our days together and wish me sweet dreams. I often wonder if I'm moving too slowly for him. If that's the way of it, it's too bad and likely not meant to be. I refuse to rush. There's been so much change in the last couple of years. I don't need another, just yet. Betsy thinks I need my head examined. Cam's the bee's knees in her opinion. She advised me to grab him with both hands and never let go.

I don't want to examine our relationship. I don't want to wonder if he's all in or not. If it happens, great. If it doesn't, I'll adjust. I don't want or need any pressure in that aspect of my life.

Are you buying that? Yeah, me neither. I think I've already fallen for him. I'm not sure if it's just weakness, need, or loneliness. Maybe it has something to do with Jake and Shirley getting married at Christmas. Could I be jealous of their unholy union?

Cindy and Brian are dreading going to the wedding. Cindy wishes that they would just elope. No one is actually talking to me about it. But, if I were asked, I would suggest that given the nature of the beginning of their relationship, elopement or the courthouse wouldn't be as classless as the fantasy of a formal wedding, as if all this were normal. It's so Jake, to expect others to bend to his will instead of considering their feelings. I'm also wondering how he can financially swing a big affair. Didn't Shirley's spending wipe him out? That's so not my business, but it is a curiosity. It wouldn't surprise me in the least to hear, last minute, that the wedding is off. After observing the betrothed couple at Thanksgiving, I could see cracks in the foundation of their relationship. An underlying argument bubbled away underneath their forced smiles and fake, cheerful demeanor.

After Shirley and Jake had said their goodbyes, they could be seen snapping at each other in the car. Aunt Millie summed it up well. From her rocking chair, she adjusted her glasses and said, "That dog won't hunt."

I appreciated her comment. With saying so little, she had said so much.

We have a new development with Brian. He's dating a little girl he met in school. Her name is Katie. She is cute as a button, a little slip of a thing, with eyes bigger than her face. She is a giggler, finds most everything amusing. Her brunette hair hits just at her tiny waist and swishes when she moves like a horse's mane.

Brian has bought himself a little Jeep, but when he takes Katie out to the movies or to the diner, he borrows my truck. He drives the Jeep to school and when he and Gil go running the roads. Hard to believe they will both be seniors in the fall of next year.

I hope Brian doesn't feel pushed to the side with all the attention that will be on Cindy and the baby. He deserves his moment in the spotlight, too. I don't want to lose what we've built. Since he has decided to start living in the bunk house, I feel like I see him less and less. I'm really glad of the influence Ranger has had in being a mentor to Brian and all the other young men. I'm glad to have them all around for the Christmas break.

I'm very excited about our plans for Christmas. We corporately decided to draw names. Also, everyone's gifts were to be handmade. I drew Betsy's name. It was a tough one. I struggled for days to think of what I could make for a woman who had most everything.

Searching the internet, I found pictures of her and Carl in various functions and charity events. Printing out the pictures and articles, I made up a scrapbook, placing the items in what I am hoping is the right chronological order. At times, I would second guess myself, hoping my gift idea won't cause her to feel grief.

We were all struggling to keep our homemade gifts a secret. More than once, I came into a room to be told "don't look." Half the fun of doing Christmas this way was the anticipation. I can hardly wait for Christmas morning!

The weeks flew by. We had some mild weather, thankfully. It was a relief for us all to see sunshine again. The animals were doing better. One of the mares, Mary, was carrying Commodore's foal. Cam said that it would come the beginning of spring. He wasn't worried about her or Martha any longer. He said she should do fine.

On Christmas morning, we woke to snow flurries. There wasn't any accumulation. You couldn't quite call it a white Christmas. Still, it was nice to see snowflakes.

After all our chores, we all gathered in the living room to exchange our gifts. Taking turns, we started with the youngest, Brian. Preston had gotten his name. As he tore open the wrapping paper, we all watched. Brian held up a whittled sling shot.

"Alright!" he hollered, causing Bill to bark.

"Keep that with you when you are out in the fields. Maybe you will scare off coyotes or wolves with it," explained Preston.

"Thanks, man." Brian rose to shake his hand. "When did you get time to make this? I didn't see you working on it at all."

"You should see our bedroom floor," Cindy said, "covered in shavings." She motioned with her hands.

Cindy opened up a crocheted hat and scarf from Aunt Millie, a beautiful set, hot pink.

Preston opened up an etched, wooden box full of cigars, made by Ranger. He nodded an approval. "I'll pass these out when little Michael is born," he bragged.

I was next. I opened a leather belt from Brian with hearts and flowers burned in a pattern. "I love it! Thank you, Brian." I rose and gave him a hug.

Ranger's gift was a drawing Cindy had made. She must have studied the entire acreage of the farm; it was very detailed. "You can take it to Alaska with you and show your family what you helped build," she told Ranger. He struggled to hide his emotions.

Betsy opened the gift from me. Tears filled her eyes as she held the scrap book to her chest.

"Oh, no!" I said. "I was afraid of that. I didn't mean to make you sad."

"I'm not sad; it's beautiful, so thoughtful. Half of this, I had forgotten about. Now, Carl will live on in memory. Thank you, it's perfect." She smiled as I breathed a sigh of relief.

Betsy had gotten Millie's name. She could hardly contain herself as she waited for Aunt Millie to peel back the wrapping. Inside the box was a note. Aunt Millie looked up in curiosity, "What in the world?" she asked. The note gave instructions for all of us to go to the road at the end of the driveway. Bundling up in our coats, Aunt Millie, Betsy, and I hopped into the cab of my truck. The rest jumped into the bed, even Bill. When we got to the top of the hill, Betsy had Aunt Millie cover her eyes. I turned the truck around, facing the farm as Betsy instructed.

"Ready? Open them," Betsy told Aunt Millie.

There it was. A beautiful hand-painted sign mounted on a decorative post. It said "Carson Hills Farm" in the center with flowers, trees, and birds surrounding the name.

"Oh, my!" exclaimed Aunt Millie. "Thank you. I love it! We are properly official now!" She clapped her hands together. Betsy gave Ranger a thumbs-up through the window.

It was a Christmas we will never forget.

Jake called late that night and talked to Cindy. As she disconnected her cell phone, she collapsed on the sofa. "The marriage is off." She looked relieved.

"What happened?" asked Brian, moving to the edge of his seat.

"It would seem that Shirley is still married to someone she knew when she was a teenager." Cindy laughed out loud. "So, she needs a divorce before they can be married."

We all looked around the room at each other. Betsy was the first to start laughing. The rest of us couldn't contain ourselves.

"That's our Shirley," I hooted.

Cam came in at that moment with a large package under his arm. "Merry Christmas, everyone. What's so funny?" This made us laugh harder. Brian relayed the whole saga of the Jake and Shirley tragedy.

"Have mercy," said Cam. "Will those two kids ever figure it out?"

Picking up his gift, the last one under the tree, I asked Cam, "Would you like to open your gift in private on the porch?" He nodded with a smile.

Sitting on the swing under a blanket, we exchanged our gifts. We had both gotten each other matching sheep skin coats. Laughing, we put on our coats and snuggled in the moonlight.

It was the perfect ending to a memorable holiday.

Chapter 39

Just when it seemed like winter would never end, we began to get warmer days. Daffodils were pushing up out of the ground. The earth was coming back to life.

Brian and Preston were watching the herd closely. They had several that were due to calve any day. The best one of them would be Brian's 4-H project for the County Fair. He was as anxious as Preston was about becoming a father, constantly checking on the progress and comfort of the cows.

Cindy looked about ready to pop. Her belly prevented her from being able to sit close enough to eat at the table. She looked so miserable, sitting alone on the couch, her plate balanced on top of her stomach. Betsy had begun to have her meals in there beside her, placing her plate on a cushion in her lap.

Cindy and Aunt Millie were on the same schedule, taking naps and early to bed. It was as if one was creating life and the other, losing the vitality of life.

Cam and I were spending more time together. I began to accompany him on calls to different farms. I enjoyed assisting him in tending to all sorts of animals. It was a learning experience as well, seeing how others manage their farms. I was getting an education in efficiency methods. I am happy too, knowing that we worked well together, in harmony with each other.

The first to be born was Mary's foal. It was a little female with Commodore's markings. Mother and baby were kept quiet in a stall for the first week, which agitated Commodore. He was the one acting like a baby, snorting and whimpering. I thought he would be more like himself when released into the field with Mary and the foal, but he basically ignored them.

We enjoyed watching the foal leap and run, kicking up her legs and stumbling into her ever patient mother. Aunt Millie wants to name her Grace. Hopefully, her little wobbly legs will grow into the name.

Next to be welcomed were the calves. They all three were born within days of each other: two males and one female. Brian chose one of the males for his 4-H project, a white-faced Hereford with a brick red coat. The white of his face was heart shaped. Brian named him Brave Heart.

Cindy was wide-eyed with wonder at seeing these births take place. She had a few questions for her doctor. I assured her that it wasn't quite the same and she would be fine.

Toward the end of May, the whole house was awakened with Cindy crying out in labor.

Preston, surprisingly calm, loaded her in their car and rushed to the hospital. Betsy and I followed closely behind. We were so excited to get the chance at holding little Michael.

I think I was moving too slowly for Betsy. Annoyed at how calm I was, she hollered, hitting the dash, "Drive it like you stole it!"

I punched it, straightening all the curves into town, while Betsy called Melissa and Mike on her cell. Their new house was closer to the hospital. We found them waiting in the lobby.

As our herd of people was parking cars, grabbing bags, and scurrying into the building, Cindy was placed in a wheelchair and whisked away to the top floor with her family camping out in the waiting room a few doors away.

Six hours later, Preston came into the room, dressed in surgical wear. Removing the hat from his head, wiping his eyes, he said, "He's here, and he is beautiful. Eight pounds and six ounces." He beamed. "Cindy is okay. They are moving us to a room; I will come back for you after we get settled. Oh, I almost forgot. Here," he said, as he passed out cigars. Betsy and I took one as well.

Melissa and Mike embraced their son.

"What's his full name, Preston?" asked Betsy, dabbing her eyes with a tissue.

He stood a little taller and held his head high. Clearing his throat for this all-important moment, he announced, "Michael Carson Powell."

The room erupted with laughter, back slaps, and clapping.

While Betsy gathered and discarded our coffee cups, napkins, and other trash we had accumulated over the duration, the rest of us gathered our belongings, readying ourselves for relocation.

A little bitty nurse came into the room and asked that we follow her.

My palms were sweating; butterflies were flapping in my stomach. I wanted to run, to see that baby boy. Talking a deep breath, I slow my steps, letting everyone else pass.

As our herd entered the room, we found Cindy propped up in bed with Preston at her side, holding her hand. Both are smiling from ear to ear. Cindy looked tired but so happy.

Little Michael is tightly swaddled in his plastic bassinet. He's really red looking and sound asleep. I can't tell much of who he looks like, he's so covered up.

"May I?" asked Melissa with her arms extended.

"You never have to ask if you want to hold your grandson, Mom," said Preston proudly.

Melissa scooped him up. Mike held up his phone to get the perfect picture of his family.

I pulled my phone out, too. These are the moments you don't want to miss.

"I want a turn," whispered Betsy. Melissa reluctantly handed him over to her.

"Now, this is the best, ever!" Betsy cried out, waking the baby. "Your turn," she said, handing him toward me.

"I'll swap you," I said, handing her my phone.

"He has your hair, Mom," said Cindy. "And your eyes." She raised her eyebrows.

He seemed so small; his little kitten cry was heartbreaking.

As I snuggled him in my arms, he stopped crying and looked up at me with dark blue eyes. Sure enough, a small sprig of auburn hair peeked from under his little cap.

I have heard the expression "took my breath away." But, I had never experienced it before this moment. Looking into the eyes of this little piece of heaven was just that, breathtaking.

In that moment, I knew I would do whatever it took to protect and nurture him for the rest of my life. I remember having this feeling with my children. The emotion was so strong, my eyes began to water. I felt such a connection with this little boy. It's as if we already knew each other, like we had met before.

"Grandpa's too?" asked Mike with his hands out. Melissa was ready to capture the moment with her phone.

Reluctantly, I handed the baby to Mike but couldn't take my eyes off him.

Cindy yawned and rubbed her eyes.

She and Preston whispered closely to each other.

"Hey, everybody, I think my wife needs rest," said Preston, with a concerned expression.

Mike handed his namesake to his son.

After a round of hugs, we slowly trickled out of the room, reluctant to leave.

"We have to prepare the house for a baby," announced Betsy.

"Yes, yes we do." I smiled back at her, already making a list in my head.

Chapter 40

Carson Hills Farm is at full tilt boogie. Spring has sprung, the ground has been turned, and it's all hands on deck for planting. Most of our machinery needed maintenance after the winter storage, but no major hiccups so far.

Betsy can be found down by the springhouse daily, checking her strawberries, looking for any hint of red. She spends much of her day spoiling little Michael. We all adore him. Cindy and Preston have lots of helping hands.

Aunt Millie seems to have a new spring in her step, pardon the pun. She loves helping with the baby, too. Her fingers may be older and bent, but she can still change a diaper with superhero like speed. The warmer weather has helped alleviate her arthritis pain.

Cindy and Preston are all in with going as natural as possible—cloth diapers, nursing, and only home-cooked, pureed food. I call it first-child syndrome. After the second one, you do what's easiest. Just saying.

Most days, the house looks like a bomb hit it. Burp cloths, clothes, and baby items are strewn on most surfaces. But no one cares or complains. Isn't it amazing that one little human can cause so much disruption?

Brian is excited for his 4-H project, pampering his bull, Brave Heart. He laughed, telling us about his dog, Bill, acting jealous, trying to get his attention when he attends to the calf. Gil has been teaching Brian about presenting at the 4-H Exhibition.

When the day of the fair opening came, we loaded everyone into Preston and Cindy's family van and followed Brian with Brave Heart in the trailer to the county fairgrounds. When I asked if his girl, Katie, would be joining us, he shrugged and changed the subject. He looked sad and a bit embarrassed. Gil let me know later that they were seeing other people. Translation: She was seeing someone else, and Brian was let down.

At the fair's livestock barn, Brian was awarded a red ribbon for second place for Best in Show. Gil took home two blue ribbons for his sheep. Brian had framed his ribbon and hung it proudly in the upstairs hallway.

It was a bit of a letdown for him to turn Brave Heart out into the field afterward. Every time Brian is working with the cattle, the little bull follows him around like a puppy.

Ranger's final days will come after the harvest in the fall. He was originally to leave after spring planting but had some difficulty with real estate paperwork. After some searching, he found some of his family in Alaska and with their help, he found a cabin.

Since I've known him, he has been a quiet person, just saying what is necessary in order to communicate. But lately, I find him to be quieter than usual. He spends most evenings sitting on the front porch with Aunt Millie. When she visits Commodore, he often accompanies her. In my thinking, it's as if he is taking a step back to let Preston become more comfortable with the responsibility of the farm. Or maybe he's saying goodbye in his own way.

Cam hasn't been around much. He says that it is the busiest time of the year with so many animals having offspring. I could buy that if he were to still call at night. I find myself missing him but glad we didn't get more serious. I'm beginning to think that the farm is my first love. It's what gets the most of my attention and time. Sure, I know it's going to hurt when he decides to break things off, but after Jake and Shirley, I think I will bounce back. This is what I tell myself; I don't know if I believe me.

As for Jake and Shirley, we haven't heard a peep. Cindy left message after message on his phone with no response. She was close to hiring a private eye to see if he had been kidnapped by Shirley's family, or worse, maybe dead in a ditch somewhere.

I had to agree with her. It wasn't like Jake to just completely disappear. With the situation, it could be that Shirley has him swaying back and forth again. Considering that she was still married to someone else, there could be foul play in the mix.

With Preston driving the tractor, Cindy and I were riding the setter, taking turns feeding starting plants into the forked placers. When Preston made a turn to start the next row, Brian came riding his four-wheeler into the field, waving his arms.

"Mom!" he shouted over the tractor motor.

Preston cut the engine off.

"It's Dad! He's in the hospital," said Brain, catching his breath. "You are still listed as his next of kin. They need your signature to treat him."

Springing into motion, I ask, "What's happened to him?"

"Not sure," answered Brian. "But it sounds serious."

Preston, pulling out his cell phone, called Ranger to tell him what was happening. Turning to us, he said that Ranger would come and relieve us.

Cindy, Brian, and I rode the four-wheeler back to the house. Grabbing my purse while Cindy explained everything to Betsy, the three of us piled into my truck and headed for the main road.

"What hospital, Brian?" I asked a little too loud as I navigated an oncoming car.

"Um, well. There's something else I probably should tell you." He hedged. "Um, Dad lives up here, now. He's at the hospital in town." He looked at me in the rear-view mirror to gage my reaction.

"That so?" I asked, trying to stay calm.

"Yep. Shirley left him for some biker dude. So, he decided to make some changes, moved his business up here and is so busy he's turning down work. What with all the people wanting to move this way for the clean country air and all the new housing from farmers selling off their land. He's rebuilding his life, said he wanted to make his kids proud of him again." His voice dwindled off at the end.

"Well, ain't that something," I stated.

"No, it's something else," said Cindy. "Why didn't he tell me?" She folded her arms.

"I'm not sure," Brian answered sincerely. "Maybe he thought you had enough going on. What with being married and having a baby and all."

"So, why is he in the hospital?" I insist.

"Seems he had an accident on one of the job sites," answered Brian.

We arrived at the hospital and went to the information desk. They sent us to the emergency room. There Jake lay, unconscious with a bandage on his head. He looked so vulnerable. But I wasn't buying it.

The attending physician approached me with paperwork. "Mrs. Cantrell, your husband is in need of surgery. He has a concussion and a compound fracture in his leg, and it requires surgery. You are listed as next of kin, and we need your signature to continue his care."

I started to explain that we aren't married any longer but decided it was just easier to sign.

He thanked me and turned to an orderly, giving him instructions.

A nurse led us to the waiting room, assuring us that Jake was in good hands.

After informing everyone at home with a phone call of Jake's situation, Cindy and I started to quiz Brian on all things Jake.

Apparently, Jake had sworn him to secrecy in fear that he would fail and have more egg on his face than usual. With the disappearance of Shirley and her biker beau, Jake had decided to do a start over of his own. Brian, with a grin, reported that Jake was envious of my ability to redo my life and a bit jealous of my success in doing so. It made more sense to him to locate near his family, even if we were no longer behaving like one. Insert more air quotes here.

Cindy was upset to be excluded from her father's decisions.

Brian continued, sorry as he could be that his sister had not been kept in the loop. The location of Jake's domicile was an abandoned firehouse in the middle of the county which he had refurbished, leaving the sliding pole and electronic doors. Some of the crew from when he had begun to rebuild his business had come with him. He was in the process of completing a subdivision that the workers would inhabit soon, moving their families to the area as well.

"He has been a busy man," I spoke with an evenness. "I know one thing he still needs."

Cindy and Brian both looked at me with raised eyebrows. "A new next of kin." Duh.

They both laughed softly.

"Mom," Brian said like a question. "I've been thinking I might like to work construction with Dad this summer. That is, well, if you can spare me from the farm."

My heart sunk a little. "Yeah, we could always hire hands. What do you think your dad will say?"

"Well." He squirmed a little. "Actually, it was his idea."

I needed air. "Sure. Couldn't hurt to learn some new skills." I stood. "Be right back."

I looked back at them as I cleared the door. Cindy was fussing at her brother.

Reaching the end of the hallway, I stared out the window to the parking lot below. I realized at that moment, I hadn't thought about Cam all day. It might be time for a conversation. We either need to get serious or move on. I'm locked in with my life; no more children for me. I'm not interested in being married again. I don't think I can handle someone having that kind of hold on me.

Hearing footsteps, I turned to see the doctor entering the room where Brian and Cindy waited.

He was in and back out before I could return.

Catching Cindy as she was coming out the door, I ask, "What did he say?"

"Dad's fine. He has a cast and is conscious. They are taking him to a room. He will be in the hospital for a few days, just to make sure there is no infection in the leg. They had to use screws to put his ankle back together." She made a face.

"Let's head home, then." I did not want to see Jake. "You two can come back later, more prepared, if you wish."

"Coward," Cindy smirked.

"No, I think you were looking for the word, avoider." I nodded.

"I think I'll just stay, if that's alright," Brian said.

Handing Cindy my keys, I ask, "Will you please get my truck from the parking lot and pick me up at the door?"

She nodded and looked over her shoulder at Brian. Then, she turned and hugged her brother before exiting down the hall.

"Brian. I love you very much. I hope these things you are doing are more for you than for your dad. I am well aware that your life can get lost in his. Been there, done that." I put my arm around him.

He looked down at me. Yes, he is taller than me now. "I want to try everything and decide what I like. Does that make sense?"

"I think that is very wise." I tip-toed, kissing his cheek goodbye. "I will send someone over with some essentials and your Jeep so you can make a getaway if need be." I winked at him before heading home.

Chapter 41

The summer has been mostly a success with the exception of losing some of our livestock to coyotes. Unfortunately, one of them was Brian's Brave Heart. I was hoping it would return him to the farm, but it only pushed him further away.

Since Brian moved in with Jake, he has been working construction all summer. Bill went with him. Being at Jake's firehouse home in town was quite an adjustment for Bill. He couldn't understand the concept of Brian sliding down the pole. Some days he would sit and bark at the pole continuously until Brian had to put him outside. Seems the construction life wasn't working for Bill either. Too many hazard areas at the job site. A dog like Bill needs to live outside and needs to work.

So, Bill became Preston's companion. We moved his doghouse from the bunk house porch to the edge of the carport next to the house. When Preston starts his day, Bill is waiting for him and works with him all day. Most of the time Bill seems quite happy. But, at the end of the day, I've observed him watching the driveway for the Jeep and the boy he loves. I wonder if Brian is missing his dog. Hopefully, he will return to us in the fall.

It's breaking my heart not having Brian here. But more than that, Ranger made an unexpected exit. He didn't even say goodbye. At the start of the workday, on a Monday, he was gone. No note, no nothing. Just gone. We called his cell phone only to hear the message, "This phone has a mailbox that hasn't been set up yet."

That night at supper, Preston confessed to knowing that Ranger was going to leave. He didn't tell us because Ranger asked him to not say anything. Preston's take on it was that if Ranger had to say goodbye, he probably couldn't have gone.

By the end of the week, we received a postcard with snowcapped mountains from Nome, Alaska, with the following words: "I couldn't bear to see your faces when I left. I hope you can forgive and understand. You are good people, and I am better for knowing you. Thank you, Miss Millie, for taking a chance on me in my youth. You all have an open invitation to visit Alaska anytime. I would relish the occasional letter, Ann. All the best, Ranger."

That's the most Ranger had ever said in one sitting.

They say these things come in threes. So, wouldn't you know it? Cam got offered a position in Texas. He would be running his own clinic. He came to the farm, hat in hand, head bowed, and made his announcement. To be honest, I wasn't that surprised. He had become distant. When I did see him, which was down to a couple of times a month, he was very quiet. As if his mind were elsewhere. I found myself repeating things I had just said to him. I had come to dread more than look forward to his visits. He wasn't the same man I had met just the year before. He tried the old line, "It's not you, it's me." Please, I know it's me.

In hindsight, never trust a fire that burns too bright after just being lit. It will die down just as quickly. My logic tells me to go for the slow building, long-lasting flame. As if I'm one to give advice.

We never said the I Love You words. I didn't say them because I didn't want to spook him. Maybe he didn't say them because he wasn't in love or loved someone else.

When he tried to explain his leaving for Texas, I told him I understood, sending him off with well wishes for success, knowing in the back of my mind that his ex-wife had relocated there. Fool me once . . . Still, my heart hurts. I'm missing Ranger, Brian, and Cam.

We've hired two local high school boys looking for summer work to take up the slack of the man shortage here at Carson Farms. I'm not sure what we will do in the fall when they return to school.

As for the women, we have thrown ourselves into our work. We take turns watching Michael and helping Preston. Michael is starting to crawl which presents a whole new set of problems. There is danger everywhere, and mother-hen Cindy is on constant alert. He could tumble down the stairs, swallow small objects, and every room has electrical outlets.

I suggested to her, perhaps that's why they make playpens. The look I received was expected.

She safety proofed the entire house. Aunt Mille is the one that had the biggest struggle; her arthritis prevents her from being able to open drawers, doors, or the gates on the exit doors. Everything—I am saying EVERYTHING—has a safety lock on it, even the bathroom toilets. Never mind that Michael could not reach them yet. Cindy's not taking any chances.

Aunt Millie had a serious talk with Cindy. No one was currently living in the bunk house. Perhaps Cindy could make it into a fortress of safety for her baby. Cindy didn't see the logic in that. To her, the bunk house was still a stinky man hut. It took Betsy stepping in to broker the peace agreement of the year. She should be considered for the Nobel Peace Prize.

Betsy's solution: all doors, drawers, and exits would remain closed when Michael was out of his crib or the playpen. Whoever was watching him would never take their eyes off him unless he was asleep in his crib or said playpen.

Reluctantly, Cindy agreed. Preston removed the safety equipment with the exception of outlet covers. That was where Cindy would not budge.

The end result of all these battles was that Preston and Cindy had the well dug and the footer poured on the property I gifted them. Jake was contracted to build their house. It would be ready to inhabit before winter. Done and dusted, as the British say.

I was happy for them. I was happy, too, that I would see more of Brian. Jake, not so much.

I was trying to keep my joy under the circumstances, but I discovered gray hair. Not just a little, but a whole streak starting from my widow's peak. I considered coloring it. But that seemed dishonest somehow. Also, I felt like the streak gave me more character.

Let's face it, I'm a divorced grandmother in her late forties with graying hair. It's not going to get better from here. I'm not a vain person. It's not about my looks. It's more like life is passing me by. All the years I wasted with Jake, then Cam comes and goes like a mighty wind. Even with Ranger, the manliest man I've ever known, gone to the final frontier. I don't know if there is someone for everyone or if there is anything to a person having at least one true love in their life, but I'm feeling like I missed the boat. Okay, enough! Pity party over.

With less help on a full-time basis, I have scaled down our production. We are concentrating on two major crops and cutting back on greenhouse projects. Our overhead has dropped considerably too.

We have reduced livestock as well, keeping just what is manageable and profitable. The mares, Mary and Martha, have gone to work at an Equine Therapy Center in Knoxville. Mary's foal, Grace, was sold to Megan Anderson. Occasionally, she rides her over from the campground to visit Cindy.

Commodore still takes morning rides with me. He is beginning to show his age. He moves slower these days and becomes irritated at Bill if he gets too close. Aunt Millie still goes to the barn for their nightly visits.

Many things make me think of Ranger. Throughout the day, I think I see him across a field or in a doorway. When I hear a truck coming down the drive, I'm still surprised it isn't his.

When the sadness gets too much, I sit down with little Michael. Running my fingers through his auburn curls gives me peace. I tickle his round belly and gaze with awe into his blazing, blue eyes. There's nothing better than little Michael cuddles to soothe me.

When he cries at night, I have to hold myself back. I'm really making an effort to stay in the grandma lane. It's especially hard when he is just a hallway away.

Fortunately, he is starting to sleep through the night. Cindy wanted to stay to a strict schedule on his nourishment. I finally convinced her to supplement at night so that he would sleep longer. With tired, red eyes, she gave me an angry look and then relented.

I haven't said I told you so. I'm just glad she took some advice.

Me, I'm too busy staring at the ceiling to sleep. I've stuck so many unanswered questions up there. Like, where do we go from here? What do I need to do next? What if? I count them like sheep until I feel the stillness take me.

Chapter 42

As Jake promised, by the end of fall, Cindy and Preston's house was completed. Built with stone pillars and wood logs, it looks like it grew right up out of the ground.

Designed with an open floor plan, it has a living area, three bedrooms, two full baths, and a front porch with a view of the valley below. From the top of the ridge behind the house, you can see the Smoky Mountains to the south and the Cumberland Gap to the Northeast. They kept a row of mature trees on the west side of the property to provide a wind break. A carport shelter stands at the top of the steep graveled driveway. Cindy finally had a home of her own.

With the last of her little family's belongings transported, Betsy and I turned to leave. We would see her tomorrow. She would be helping in the fields while Betsy watched Michael.

As Preston passed us carrying Michael in his car seat, he said tiredly, "I think that's it."

We watched as he settled Michael on the porch and scooped Cindy up in his arms. "Woman, I am carrying you over the threshold."

Cindy squealed. "Pres, we have been through that door a zillion times."

"Ah, young love," sighed Betsy.

We linked arms and headed to my truck. The new, loose gravel on their driveway crunched under my tires. We were back to the now empty house within five minutes. Aunt Millie was clearing away dishes from the rushed supper we had before taking the last load to Cindy and Preston's.

"It will be strange to not have them here, under the same roof." She sighed.

Betsy and I both silently nodded in agreement.

"Brian, too," said Betsy with a sigh of her own.

"How on earth did we manage to run off all the males in this place?" I asked, horrified.

They both just shrugged. "It will be okay, we just need to adjust to it." I attempted a smile at them.

"Yeah?" asked Betsy. "Better tell that to your face," she teased.

After spending some time staring into the two now empty bedrooms, previously occupied with my family members, I put myself to bed.

With the sweet surrender of sleep alluding me, I decided to write Ranger a letter. In it, I poured out my heart. I told him how lonesome the place was without him and Brian, about how we had to scale back considering our lack of hands. I explained the situation with Jake and the abandonment of Cam. I wanted him to know how I felt about Brian, Preston, Cindy, and little Michael moving out. I all but told him that even the fence posts miss him. By the time I had finished my letter, it was three pages long. Part of me wanted to wad it up and toss it in the trash, but I wouldn't because it was honest and made me feel better just to tell him about what life here was like without him. Maybe I was laying a guilt trip on him. Maybe I was just wishing I could hear him tell me it would all be okay.

It did help me sleep. So, I kept writing. Every night, I would spend some time pretending I was talking to Ranger just like we did before his leaving.

Somehow, we would get through this transition. We would all be okay. At the end of each week, I mailed what I had written, never hearing back from him.

Thanksgiving came, and still not a word from Ranger. We had the usual people show up.

Bond Wilson was absent this year. He had fallen for a schoolteacher over the summer. This brought me much relief. I hope it would for Ranger, too, considering their history.

It was fun to have little Michael around for the holidays. He really brightened up things.

There was no conflict like we had the year before.

Even my parents and Jake were on their good behavior. I was thinking maybe I had misjudged my mother. She could have only wanted to see her daughter settled, happy, and established. That idea was not long lived. Across a plate with just the tiniest sampling of each dessert, she made "helpful" suggestions on my hair, makeup, and clothes. After all, we need to keep up appearances to get and keep a man. My reaction to her nitpicking was borrowed from Cindy. "Whatever."

Jake and Brian were enthusiastic about how the construction business was booming and about Brian's senior year plans. I was more interested in his after-graduation plans.

He was a step ahead of me. It looked like the construction business was more to his liking than farming. Even seeing Bill again didn't have any pull. Something I had forgotten was dogs will love whoever feeds them. I guess that makes Bill mostly mine.

Fortunately, Aunt Millie's daughter, son, and his family made it for Thanksgiving. It was good to see them all, especially for Aunt Millie. We had a great time laughing over their childhood memories. Time seemed to pass so quickly and before we were ready, they hurried off back to their lives. Aunt Mille pleaded but couldn't convince them to stay any longer.

The morning after Thanksgiving, Betsy was on a mission to bring Christmas cheer to the farm. She had a chore list for each of us.

"We are not going to mope about anymore!" she exclaimed. "Enough! We are getting our Christmas joy on."

"Yes, boss," I saluted her. My job was finding the perfect tree, exactly six feet tall.

This meant going into Ranger's trees. Preston had kept them cleared out by bush hogging. So, it shouldn't be too difficult.

After getting the chain saw out of the shed, I checked it for fuel and oiled the teeth. Putting it into the truck bed along with a few other tools, I climbed into the cab and began to meander my way over the hills. Opening and closing several gates, I finally reached the field full of evergreens.

Sidestepping around the new saplings, I spot the perfect tree. Using my measuring tape, I find it's too tall. Resuming my search, I hear a sound behind me. Knowing it could be a coyote, bear, or mountain lion, I chide myself for not bringing a rifle with me. If I could just make it back to the safety of the truck.

Just then I hear Bill yelp a greeting. "Hey, Buddy. Want to help me find a good tree?" I asked, relieved.

A figure appeared at the top of the hill. The sun was behind the figure, so I couldn't quite make out who it was. Shielding my eyes, I thought, *No, it's not possible.*

He removed his hat. Was it, could it be, am I imagining him? It was Ranger. I was flooded with emotion. I ran to him.

Just as I reached him, I slowed my pace, taking in all of him from head to toe. He looked thinner, some age to his face, and with a bit of gray in his jet-black hair.

"Oh, Ranger. You are a sight to see. I thought you were a figment of my imagination. But you're really here. Right in front of me." I cupped my hands to my face in disbelief. "But wait," I paused. "Why are you here? What about Alaska?" I backed away, waiting, my heart pounding. "What about your people, the family you were looking for?" Embarrassment of the intimacy of my letters flooded through me. I became still, trying to shrink into the pasture.

Bill sat next to him, looking up at us, probably wondering what the humans were doing.

"Ann," he whispered, saying my name with such tenderness. "Your letters, they made me realize that I couldn't settle there. This land, it's where I belong, not in some far away cabin, alone. But here, where you are. You are my people."

"You're home, welcome home!" I jumped toward him, wrapping my arms around him in a bear hug. "Oh, I'm sorry," I said, catching myself, stepping back.

"No sorry needed. It's the best thing that's happened to me, well, in a long time." He smiled, crinkling his eyes. "Now, I believe we have a tree to cut down. I know just the one."

Crooking his elbow, he offered me his arm. I linked my arm in his.

That was the beginning.

We were starting over, something we both knew how to do. Isn't that what life is, just a series of starting over again and again? Only, this time, I wasn't doing it alone.

Epilogue

It's been ten years since we welcomed Ranger back home. The farm came back to life with him there. We had many successes and some failures but have managed it well enough to be productive.

I think Aunt Millie would be proud of our success. Carson Farms has become a destination for weddings with ceremonies in the high pasture and receptions in the barn. Mostly, I think she would be proud that we have kept family in the business and taught agriculture to the younger generations.

Cindy and Preston are still going strong and have added a little girl to their family. Her name is Elizabeth, but we call her little Betsy because she has the attitude and confidence of her namesake. Michael adores his little sister. Like a shadow, she follows him everywhere. He only complains when she asks questions beyond his patience.

Cindy is continuously coming up with new ideas to generate income on the farm. She has a hard time when someone doesn't agree with her creativity but has gotten better at letting things go. Her idea of a bed and breakfast hasn't returned. Her family and the farm keep her too busy.

Brian has taken over Jake's business. He is yet to marry. We get hopeful when he brings a new love interest around for us to meet but have learned to not get too attached. He could be over the moon about someone and next thing we know, it's ended.

Jake has retired and spends his days golfing, of all things. Who knew he liked to golf? He still advises Brian about the business. He dates around with no steady lady friend. He's probably still gun shy from the Shirley experience. No one knows Shirley's whereabouts. She is likely gone with the wind.

Surprisingly, Bond Wilson has not only gotten married to the school-teacher he was seeing, but also he has three daughters and another on the way. He's gone bald too. Poor guy is too tired to even flirt with anyone else. Karma strikes again.

We get together with Preston's parents, Mike and Melissa, as often as possible. We watch ball games, have movie nights, game nights, and meals after church on Sundays. Mike had a scare with his heart, but with Melissa's care, has recuperated. She watches his diet and exercise routine like a hawk.

We lost Aunt Millie last year. She, blessedly, died in her sleep. Her funeral was something else. I didn't know there were that many people in this county. The crowd was so large, we had to move the service outside. Many shared about how she had touched their life. I miss her every day, but it is getting easier to learn how to live with the grief. I feel her with me when I'm doing a chore or walking the land. Sometimes I talk to her. It helps ease the ache of missing her.

Poor Betsy was heartbroken, but the care of little Elizabeth gave her a welcome distraction. She is teaching her to dance, sew, cook, sing, and do practical jokes. They are like a comedy duo.

Commodore and Bill have both been gone for several years now. We have brought in more rescue horses to rehabilitate and a rescue dog, Lucy. She's a mutt, but she is great with the livestock and a good companion to us all.

We have feral cats living in the barn. We aren't sure where they came from. They just showed up one cold winter's day. Betsy and Elizabeth gave them names, Cleopatra and Brutus. I don't think Brutus is a boy, but does it really matter?

My parents remain unchanged. When my mother went into an assisted living facility, my father went with her. They have lived there for around a year now. I try to visit them most Saturdays. It's easier to visit with my mother now. Sadly, she has Alzheimer's. She doesn't admonish me about anything. My father never leaves her side. That's the way he wants it, so I have to accept it. Any day, I will get the call that she is gone. He might be going soon after, following her lead as usual.

Ranger and I were married the next year after his return. I am so glad we didn't wait too late to have our start over. We had a quiet ceremony at the house and honeymooned at a bed and breakfast in Cumberland Gap. We work so well together. There are no head games, yelling, or petty arguments. When we disagree, we reason it out and meet each other somewhere in the middle. He thinks I'm awesome, which surprises me every day because I think he's the cat's pajamas too. It's wonderful to be truly loved and to be in love.

My best wish for anyone is that you hear those two kind words from someone special in your life: welcome home. To have both a home and people there who love you is the definition of success and victory over any hardship endured during your life path.

Acknowledgments

First, I would like to give my appreciation to my friend and neighbor, Eunice Turner. Thank you for your efforts in editing my first draft and for always being so kind and thoughtful.

Secondly, I'm thankful to my family members that weren't afraid to take on a little girl, to protect her, care for her, and teach her. What little I know of farming comes from a nice parcel of land in Claiborne County, where as a child I lived with my grandparents, Millard and Roxie Killion. Upon their retirement, the farm was purchased by my uncle and aunt, Bradley and Lucille Keck. The summers my brother, Eddie, and I spent there with my cousins, Dale and Anita, were the best parts of my childhood.

After uncle Bradley passed away, aunt Lucille ran the farm for a while until she faced many physical limitations. Since aunt Lucille's passing, my cousin, Dale, and his wife, Kathy, have taken on the responsibilities. The farm has remained in the family. I'm ever so thankful for them both.

Last, but certainly not least, I am thankful for my husband, Ken, as well as other family members and friends for their encouragement, patience, and understanding while I was telling Ann's story of struggle and hope.

May all that read this book hear those warm words of love and acceptance in their lifetime, *Welcome Home*.

About the Author

Rita Rumgay grew up in both the city and the country. She currently lives in Knoxville, Tennessee with her husband, four sons, daughter in law, and granddaughter. After working various jobs since age 14, then graduating from Pellissippi Technical Community College in 2005, she is currently enjoying retirement. Her days are spent gardening, catching up on home projects, writing, and spending time with her beloved family and special pets. Her first book, *Rainbow Bridge*, published by Jan-Carol Publishing, Inc., can be found on Amazon.com. *Welcome Home*, her second book, was inspired by the question, "What If?"—where would a different life choice have taken you?

Her next book, *The Squirrel that Wore Overalls*, will be written with her granddaughter and illustrated by her daughter-in-law, a real family affair!

You can find her on Facebook and on her website that will be launched in 2023, www.ritarumgay.com. Until then, happy reading!